Dear Reader,

There are times when everything seems to be going well.

Don't be frightened. It won't last.

I got the idea for this story during one of those rare moments when I arrogantly thought I could accomplish one of my goals. It was at that exact moment of total self-satisfaction when life stepped in and slapped me with a ripe tomato…thank you very much.

I like to think I can roll with the punches, but most of the time it's more of a heavyweight championship. When goals come too easily, it makes me uncomfortable. I tend to crave the challenge, or else, what's the point?

That's why I brought Mya and Eric together. It seemed only right that they should battle it out and come to the only reasonable conclusion… well, I can't tell you that conclusion here. You'll simply have to read the book.

Please come visit me at www.maryleo.net. We'll talk more.

Enjoy the tomatoes.

Best,

Mary Leo

*So there they stood,
arms locked around each other like
they were old friends, buddies,
soul mates, or even lovers.*

To the world they were just another kissing couple at the airport.

However, Mya had a different take on the whole thing. Hers was more of the startled variety. Such as, when out of a crowd of people, a stranger calls your name and you try your best to recognize this person.

Okay, it wasn't quite like that, but it should have been for all the contact she'd had with Eric over the years. Let's see, the last real memory Mya had of him was when they were seven years old and he had just thrown a huge bucket of water over her sand castle. Of course, she had retaliated by wrecking *his* sand castle by bulldozing it with her sweet little feet.

She had seen pictures of him at various stages of growth and accomplishment, but who can keep up with all that changing? She was too busy with her own life to worry about Eric's—he had just been the boy who tormented her and whom she loved to torment back.

Now Mya didn't know what to say—which absolutely, positively never happened to her. Yet here she was in the arms of Eric Baldini, who, for some odd reason, made her pulse quicken and, for a brief moment, seemed enormously sexy.

A Pinch of Cool

Mary Leo

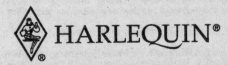

HARLEQUIN®

TORONTO • NEW YORK • LONDON
AMSTERDAM • PARIS • SYDNEY • HAMBURG
STOCKHOLM • ATHENS • TOKYO • MILAN • MADRID
PRAGUE • WARSAW • BUDAPEST • AUCKLAND

ISBN 0-373-44210-6

A PINCH OF COOL

www.eHarlequin.com

Printed in U.S.A.

ABOUT THE AUTHOR

A Pinch of Cool is Mary Leo's third novel. She's had careers as a salesgirl in Chicago, a cocktail waitress and Keno runner in Las Vegas, a bartender in Silicon Valley and a production assistant in Hollywood. She has recently given up her career as an IC Layout Engineer to pursue her constant passion: writing romance.

Mary now lives in Pennsylvania with her husband and new puppy.

Books by Mary Leo

HARLEQUIN FLIPSIDE
7—STICK SHIFT
18—FOR BETTER OR CURSED

I've been blessed to have known
quite a few extraordinary women in my life,
but none of them have impressed me more, been
as plucky, made me laugh, guided me, inspired
me, shown as much courage, and ultimately been
as cool as Katina Resann. This book,
my flamboyant friend, is dedicated to you.

1

"MOM, DON'T CRY. I hate it when you cry," Mya Strano said into the phone. Her mother had called bright and early on a Monday morning in April, just to *chat*, but there had been very little chatting. Just that silent thing mixed in with heavy sighing and runny-nose sounds, which only meant one thing. Tears.

"Who said I was crying?" Rita Strano spluttered.

Denial, that was the key. Always a clue to her mom's true emotions.

"I can hear it in your voice."

"A person can't hear tears."

"Believe me, Mom. I could hear your tears in my sleep."

"How you talk."

It was one thing to hear a friend cry, or see a co-worker cry, or watch tears stream down Cher's face in a movie. *Why is it that she never got a red nose? Some people have all the luck.* But when your own mother cried, it was almost surreal. Like, it couldn't possibly be happening. *Not to my mom.*

Mothers weren't supposed to cry, at least not on the phone to their daughters. The whole mother-daughter system wasn't set up for such episodes. It threw the world off balance, blew the stars out of the sky, and made twenty-six-year-old daughters want to hurl themselves down flights of stairs for lack of knowing what to do to stop it—a completely unstable act, but acceptable given the extreme circumstances.

"Okay. So maybe I'm upset." *Ah, an admission. The first step in the order of things.* "But who wouldn't be? We've made that network more money than anybody else and just because we're slipping a little…"

The knot in Mya's stomach began to unwind, and she could forgo the stair hurling. A ray of light had beamed in through the tunnel of despair, or something equally as metaphorical.

"Mom, how far are you slipping?"

Mya gazed at her light gray cubical walls and waited for the answer. *This might take a while.* The walls were littered with local fashion ads, mostly from SoHo, up-scale restaurant logos, and pictures of New York street vendors. She especially liked the street vendors. Some of those guys were really cute in an entrepreneurial sort of way. There was something sexy about a guy who depended on his ability to pitch to make his living that was exciting to her. Not that she'd go off and have an affair with one of them. Not really. Okay, there was that one artist in Times Square who hocked those cute little cigar-box purses—so totally out now—but he didn't count. He was actually an intellectual, *caught up in society's intolerance of the struggling artist.*

All right, so she fell for the line, and until she came to her senses, they'd had a great time together…that one night, when he gave her all the purses, then left for Toledo to take over his father's plumbing business. But that was ancient history, when she'd first arrived in the city. Something like that could never happen again, she told herself as her feet rested on a recently delivered carton of I Heart N.Y. T-shirts.

"Minor details," her mother finally said.

"What?" Could her mother now hear her inner musings? Had she gone psychic?

"Stay with me, dear. Our ratings should be minor details to the network. We still get a ton of fan mail."

Oh, yeah, crying mothers. "Mom, the network doesn't care about fan mail. They only care about ratings."

"Fickle bastards."

Mya sat back in her Aeron—ergonomically chic chair. She thought she should simply get used to these mom-tears. They weren't for anything catastrophic like a relative dying or a mile-long meteor heading for earth, although, to her mom, low ratings ranked right up there with a good blight, or the ever popular imploding sun.

Mya's mother, Rita, and Franko Baldini, Rita's longtime business partner and sometimes lover, were the stars of a network cooking show, *La Dolce Rita*. The show had been on the air for nine straight years. Lately, however, the show was hitting a dry spell, and her mother seemed to get all weepy about it almost every time Mya spoke with her. Only this time Mya was determined to do something, despite her mother's inability to accept help.

"Mom, tell me what I can do for you."

"You can be happy you're not on TV. It's a competitive, young world and I'm getting too old for it. You get one lousy wrinkle and they want to take you off the air."

Her mom let out a long sob. It was simply too much. Mya wished she could be there to cheer her up, but Rita lived in Los Angeles and Mya now lived in New York City, a move she was beginning to…she couldn't even think it…okay, a move she was beginning to regret. *God, now I'm going to start crying.*

She sat up straight and reined in her tearful thoughts. "That's not true. Look at Emeril. He has wrinkles."

"He's a man, dear."

"Okay, so Emeril's not a good example, but age has nothing to do with your ability to cook and entertain."

"Tell that to my producers. They probably want to replace Franko and me with a couple of teenagers in tight miniskirts and purple hair. I bet they're even talking to Paris Hilton. Maybe if I dye my hair blond, and get a face-lift and wear designer clothes—"

"That's it," Mya announced after taking a swig of her raspberry-mocha low-fat latte. Her mother had come up with the perfect way for Mya to help.

"You want me to get a face-lift?"

"Not you, silly. The show. *La Dolce Rita* needs a face-lift and I'm the girl to give it one."

"But how—"

Mya felt that rush of excitement she lived for. She absolutely loved to plan, and do, and make over. It was her passion to find the latest trend and bring it into focus. Actually, it was her job at NowQuest, a trend analysis boutique in the ultra-cool, significantly hip SoHo. Mya was addicted to cool in a way that only another trend spotter could understand. She woke up each morning and skimmed four big-city newspapers, watched MTV and the Style Network for countless hours, read hundreds of magazines, traveled with a small video camera, her laptop, a Polaroid, a picture-taking cell phone and started up conversations with strangers—hence the T-shirts and cigar-box purses—just to see what they were thinking. Mya was an information omnivore and reveled in every aspect of it.

"Here's the thing. Somebody has to fly out to Vegas for a client, so I'm thinking I'll volunteer, but I'll start the fact-seeking odyssey in L.A. with you and Franko. It should only take me about a week, maybe two at the most to get your show all hipped up." *A new set with a hot band, and maybe some guest appearances.* "My head's already whirling with ideas. I've got a buildup of vacation hours, so my boss won't care. Then I'll hop on over to Vegas, get our client all happy, take in a show or two—a girl's gotta have fun—and fly back here with my research. How's that?"

Her mother didn't respond. Not really. It was more in the form of someone trying to get over a crying spell, with that breathy sound kids get when they want your attention. Apparently, her mother needed a bit more coaxing.

"Mom, you know you want me to do this."

"Will I have to dye my hair pink?"

"Only if you want to, but pink hair is way out. A deep auburn might be nice, but I'll check it out and let you know. It might be the Diane Keaton look, or maybe that was last year. We may add some sassy highlights just to give it that extra drama."

Silence.

"Mom? Are you there? You can cook for me every day if you want. Fattening foods, like rice pudding with real cream and a pound of sugar. I'll even gain some weight for you. C'mon, Mom. Let me at least pitch the ideas to you. If you don't like 'em, you can hire some new agent to needle your producers, but please let me try."

Mya glanced at the Hello Kitty clock on her desk. She had exactly ten minutes to get to a meeting about that very Vegas client, and she hadn't even looked at her notes yet.

More silence.

"Mom. Say something, please."

Mya pulled out her notebook on Blues Rock Bistro, the client whom she and her entire company were trying to convince to change their image in order to open a Las Vegas hotel and casino. So far, Blues Rock was interested, but they still hadn't signed on the bottom line.

She skimmed her notes while her mother spoke. "If you really think you can help, then who am I to stop you?"

"Is that a yes?"

"Maybe you're just what we need to get our ratings back into the top ten."

"Great!" Mya opened her calendar on her ultra-thin laptop screen and skimmed her appointments. Her days were booked solid, but her evenings sucked. Not one real date. "I can be there a week from Thursday."

"I have a meeting with the producers this Friday. I'd love it if you could be here for the meeting. I'm feeling especially vulnerable these days and I couldn't take it if the meeting didn't go well. I think I need all the support I can get."

Like that is even remotely possible. How on earth did her mother expect her to be there by Friday? And with a presentation? She couldn't possibly—

More sniffling.

"I'll fly in this Thursday afternoon, but you have to

agree to let me do this my way, or it won't work. Actually, I've always wanted to—"

"Sounds fab, dear. I'll send a limo to pick you up at LAX. Just phone me with the details. See you Thursday, sweetie. Bye-ee."

And just like that, all was right in the world of daughters and mothers. There would be no hurling today.

THURSDAY, AT EXACTLY twelve noon, Mya strapped herself into the comfy leather window seat on Jet Blue's A320 Airbus. She loved to fly Jet Blue. It was by far the coolest airline on the planet with its private in-flight TV shows and roomy aisles.

There was something grand about the thrust of a jet engine. Sexual. Erotic. Titillating. *Am I horny or what?*

Anyway, she liked the sound of it. The power of being propelled through the air above the earth. The wonder of looking down over the ocean and the city beneath her feet. Or maybe she was just excited about the whole concept of getting a mini-vacation and getting the hell out of the city for a while. It's not that she didn't love New York, she did, on Sundays and most holidays, but Mya Strano was a California girl at heart, and nothing could change that.

Okay, so there were a few things she liked about the city. Her upscale apartment in the Village, her coffee shop on the corner, not to mention the fabulous nightlife and the fact that her friends were some of the coolest people in Manhattan, or so they said.

And the men she had admitted to dating, she'd kept the street vendors on the DL, were so perfectly cool that occasionally she'd have to break up with them just to see if the separation genuinely hurt. Most of the time, it hadn't. Not really.

Not that she hadn't actually felt emotion for a few of them. She had, but most of the guys hadn't been able to feel any real emotion in return. Which would have been fine if she were a rock, but seeing as how she had flesh and bones and a beating heart, she wanted something a little more emotionally satisfying.

At least that's why she had broken it off with totally cool, and totally full of himself, Bryan Heart. He was by far the hipster of all hipsters. The Brad Pitt of her fashion-obsessed world, but after he told her that he couldn't let himself fall in love with her until it was cool to be in a relationship, she had to end it. The irony was that as he walked away, he told her not to worry, because as soon as relationships were back in again, she'd be first on his call-back list.

That was over a year ago and she was still waiting for his call.

So, all right, she had a thing for radically cool guys. *Could be worse!*

But that wasn't her only problem with living on her own and running with the *in* crowd. The transition from one coast to another had been an almost insurmountable task.

It was probably the one thing in Mya's nearly perfect life that somewhat confused her. Of course, she blamed this malady on the weather more than anything else. Mya wasn't used to all that cold, and wind, and snow, sleet, ice, rain and outrageous humidity that could melt a girl's skin right off her sexy little body. She was more the sunshine and occasional earthquake kind of chick, and all that other stuff was way over the top.

The thing was, Mya wasn't a quitter. Not ever. Nothing deterred her when she was on a quest for success.

Two years ago, Mya had decided that twenty-four was way too old to be living at home and living off of Mom, so she packed up her stuff to make her way in the world. Start her own life. Find her passion. Make her mark.

Anyway, that world was New York City, where she landed the absolute coolest job a girl could have. On a scale of cool dream jobs, it had to rank number one. But that was two years ago. Now, she missed her family, and the beach, with all those cute surfer-type guys, and maybe a little of that California nightlife, and well, maybe she just needed to go home for a while. To let her mother dote on her. Cook for her.

All right, so she missed being pampered. Who wouldn't with a mother like hers? Rita was one of those fifties moms who cooked a real breakfast every morning and darned socks. *And let me tell you, my socks can use some darning.*

But what was even better than darned socks and sunshine was the fact that she was flying home to help her mother fix a problem that Mya was crashingly certain she could solve.

Mom and Franko were on a downward spiral to oblivion. When Mya had checked, their ratings were falling right through the proverbial floor, and Mya was only too happy to turn that trend around. She was the queen of finding the tipping point, and loved the challenge of searching out the latest cool, then applying it to a struggling business. Mya knew about cool from the moment she started coordinating her own Care Bear outfits while she was busy learning how to walk. It was only appropriate for her to recreate her mother's show and add some raw *wow!* to the pot.

Mya spent the entire flight to L.A. in her own little world of *au courant*. She had her laptop purring with ideas for the set, their clothes, the food and the whole feel of the show. She cross-referenced various reports on popular cooking magazines and interviews with top chefs and various well-known foodies. Then she added a couple of opinion reports from teenage hipsters, and data from Vegas strippers—they were the latest trendsetters.

She momentarily flashed on erecting a pole in her apartment, but then thought how pathetic it would be if she never had the opportunity to use it. She'd have to hire somebody to have it taken out and even her neighbors would know that she had no sex life. Of course, she could probably find a cute street vendor to do a pole dance for her, then she could keep it.

Could I be more of an embarrassment to myself?

Never mind all that, Mya had a keen eye for cool no matter what the venue.

There was only one little pesky problem on Mya's overflowing plate of things to do…her boss, Grace Chin, a delightful woman, who should have been happy for Mya.

However, Grace hadn't reacted quite the way Mya had expected. It was more of a reaction in the category of popping a vein when Mya had told her she was combining a vacation with her business trip to Vegas.

No worries. Mya had both the new client's research and her mother's revamp succinctly under control and ready for total *buzz* liftoff.

Mya was almost giddy about five hours later as she stepped off the plane and made her way over to Baggage inside LAX. She lifted her checkered orange-and-pink French luggage off the baggage carrousel with absolute abandon and walked right out the glass doors and even though it was raining, she knew it wouldn't last. That was the thing about L.A., the rain only had a bit part.

Mya actually hummed that old song about how it never rained in Southern California, as she happily pulled her bags over to the side to wait under the overhang for the limo her mother had promised to send.

Not to worry.

Hum. Hum. Hum. It was only a matter of time before the limo driver would pull up looking for her. He might even hold up a sign with her name written on it, and she would be whisked away in the back seat of plush luxury, humming as the driver maneuvered the crowded streets of one of America's finest cities.

Hum. Hum. Hum.

Mya stared at the endless stream of gnarled traffic trying to get past security and cops while the rain continued to fall. A chill swept over her. For a brief instant, she wished she'd been smart enough to pull a sweater out of her bag, but the instant passed when she saw a limo heading right for her.

Right on time...well...almost, but who cares?

Mya began to pull her luggage up to the curb when the limo stopped a few yards away and the driver got out.

"I'm over here," she called, while waving her arms. She now stood out in the rain. She thought maybe the driver couldn't see her. After all, the airport was extremely busy, so she began to walk toward him. Just then, a Chinese family of four approached the limo and the driver opened the back door.

"Wait! That's my car!" she yelled, but no one paid the slightest bit of attention to her. When the family was safely tucked inside, and all the luggage, red Samsonite, was loaded in the trunk, the driver hopped back in the front seat and drove away…in Mya's limo, no doubt.

The question of the moment was: How could the driver mistake a Chinese family for Mya? Could he be that stupid?

Okay, so apparently that wasn't my limo, but where is it?

She told herself to relax. Take a deep breath. Slowly let it out. Count to ten, or twenty, or one million. Something. Anything to relax.

She rolled her luggage back under the overhang and waited.

So, maybe her plane was a little early getting in, which would explain why *her* limo hadn't arrived yet, plus getting through all that security stuff had to take a long time.

It started to rain harder and Mya, wearing nothing but a sleeveless sundress, purple ankle socks and brown heels started to shiver.

There's no shivering in California.

She pulled a long strand of golden-red hair off her face, and wrapped her arms across her chest for some warmth. All right, perhaps it was raining a little more and a little longer than she had expected. Not something to worry about. Her limo would arrive at any moment, and the driver would probably bring a warm towel for her to dry off with.

Could happen.

She pulled her cell phone out of her cigar-box purse. Hey, with some fifty purses to choose from, a girl's gotta find one she likes, even if they were so last year.

She phoned her mom's cell.

No answer. She wanted to leave a message, but her mother had never figured out how to retrieve them, so why bother.

Mya had left precise flight information with her mother, even faxing the itinerary as a backup. She just didn't understand where that damn limo could be.

She called Franko.

Of course, there was no answer. He didn't like cell phones so he never had it with him. She pictured his poor little lonely phone stuck in a drawer somewhere just ringing and ringing.

"Okay, I've reached my crazy point," she said out loud.

After waiting a good twenty minutes, with the rain still coming down, and no limo in sight, total frustration took over and Mya decided to simply take a cab.

Just as she was about to call her mom and tell her the new plan, she noticed an old beat-up van idling off to the right. There was something white taped up to the side window. When she looked harder, her name was scribbled in big black letters on a piece of white paper.

Now what?

Her mind whirled with scenarios. Maybe things were worse at home than she'd thought. Maybe her mother had lost all her money in some bad cooking deal and the only thing she could afford was a used van. A white used van, with Georgia plates.

"No wonder she's always crying."

The woman in the obviously warm raincoat standing next to her threw Mya a nasty look and moved away.

"Fine," Mya called after her. "You should move away from me. I'm even scaring myself."

Mya knew she was having ridiculous thoughts, but the van had her name on it. That in itself was ridiculous.

She didn't quite know if she should actually approach the van, or stay as far away from it as possible, but she was desperate to get home and out of the rain. She decided to check it out, just in case her mother was inside, hiding from a potential press scandal.

She gingerly stepped out from under her shelter and into the rain again, hoping this was worth it. She walked right up to the Georgian treasure, and looked inside. It actually had a foul odor wafting out through an open side window. She backed away, holding her nose.

Whoa! Mom, what have you got in there?

The van was even worse than she could have imagined. Her mother couldn't possibly own it. There wasn't any stove.

Mya peeked in a side window, putting her face right up to the glass, but she didn't see anybody. Empty cans and jars, clothes and some very expensive-looking professional video equipment littered the inside. There were only two bucket seats in the front. Everything else had been ripped out.

Wait.

Somebody or something moved in the very back of the van. She couldn't make out if it was man or beast because the lighting wasn't quite right. She cupped her hand around her eyes to shield out any backlighting.

That's when a white flash of huge teeth, attached to

a head the size of an adult bear, growled and leaped right at her. Mya jumped back, screamed and fell right out of her Miu Miu heels, landing in a nice warm puddle.

"Damn!"

"Voodoo, sit," a male voice said from behind her.

"Excuse me?" Mya said.

The crazed animal inside the van immediately sat down, but the barking didn't stop.

Mya wanted to run for her life, but her cute little shoes sat right in front of the dreaded van. She refused to leave without her new shoes. They pulled her entire outfit together.

"I was talking to my dog," he said as he stood in front of her offering his hand to help her up.

"I knew that," she told him, trying for some calculated sarcasm.

She didn't want his help. Instead, she stood up all on her own, and even though she was now entirely drenched, with a very wet bottom, she still had her dignity. Kind of.

"That animal is vicious," Mya shouted. "He should be put down. Destroyed. What's the matter with you leaving him in there to scare somebody to death?"

"He's very protective of his home. He must have thought of you as a threat," the Voodoo owner offered.

Mya could barely see him. Her bangs covered her eyes, but from what little she could make out, he looked somewhat familiar. Unfortunately, she didn't have time to figure out where she'd met him before.

"Me? A threat? To whom?" she asked.

"To me?"

"To you! Somehow I think it's the other way around."

"Why? I wasn't the one who was peeking in windows. They have laws for that you know."

He had a point, but Mya was never going to admit she was actually looking for her mother in that junk heap.

The rain eased to a drizzle, and when Mya finally got a good look at him he was almost cute, with golden-chestnut hair—somewhat curly—and piercing gray-green eyes and a slight grin on his lips. He had a fairly large nose with a slight roundness to the tip, but it fit his boyish face, and if he were cleaned up, he might actually be handsome…in that nerdy, street vendor sort of way. The man desperately needed a shave. Not that facial hair was bad. As a matter of fact, it was coming back in, but it had to be kept neat under the chin. His wasn't. And his hair could have used a trim, much too long, with ringlets surrounding his face and ears. Of course, he had an amazing build under that wrinkled blue parka he wore, *but who's looking*.

SO THE GUY *was a hot nerd*. It's not like she was going to start dancing around a pole or anything. Oh wait, she didn't have a pole…yet.

"I wasn't peeking in your window," Mya corrected.

"Oh?" He stood there staring at her from his six-foot-something vantage point, his arms folded up tight across his chest. Glaring.

All right, so she had a thing for tall guys, seeing as how she was a mighty five foot five, but they had to be tall, *cool* guys, and this one totally lacked the cool part. He would simply never do.

She immediately stopped herself from staring. "Well, all right. Maybe I was, but not the way you mean. I was merely trying to see who was inside."

"And the reason being?"

Did he ever stop with the questions?

He was enough to infuriate her normally calm disposition. She folded her arms across her chest as well.

"You have my name taped to your window. I suspect you were mistakenly sent here by my mother."

"Holy shit! Mya? Mya Strano? It's me. Eric. Franko's son. Eric Baldini. Don't you remember me?"

That evil little boy had grown up, and now he drove a piece of junk and owned a killer dog and as incredible as it seemed, he was there to give her a ride home.

Holy shit!

2

So THERE THEY STOOD, arms locked around each other like they were old friends, buddies, soul mates or even lovers. To the world humming around them they were just another kissing couple at the airport, with one of them either going or coming.

However, Mya had a different take on the whole thing. Hers was more of the startled variety. One of those times when out of a crowd of people a stranger calls out your name and you try your best to recognize this person who says he or she knows you.

Okay, it wasn't quite like that, but it should have been for all the contact they'd had over the years. Let's see, the last real memory Mya had of Eric, they were seven years old and he had just thrown a huge bucket of water over her sand castle, completely destroying it, on a beach in Malibu. Of course, she had retaliated by wrecking his sand castle by simply bulldozing over it with her sweet little feet.

Yes, and over the years she had seen pictures of him at various stages of growth and accomplishments, but who can keep up with all that growing and changing? She was too busy with her own hormones and accolades to worry about Eric's, the boy who tormented her and she loved to torment back.

Eric had moved to Georgia, *now the plates make sense,* with his mother after his dad and mom had divorced. Even when it had come time to say goodbye to him, *which was actually at this very airport,* she had stuck out her tongue in defiance. No hugging. No tears. Not even a handshake. Not that seven-year-olds are known for shaking hands, but they could have done something. *He could have done something.* They never even touched… of course, there was that time out by the green shed when they were playing double-dare, but she didn't want to think about that now. She was too busy hugging a childhood memory.

Oh wait, she suddenly remembered that they did hold hands in the airport, for a moment, but that didn't count. They were merely both playing with his ticket when their hands touched. A natural accident.

She had been silly with joy when he moved away. At least for the first few weeks. Then she had missed their arguments and missed having him around to play with. She'd gotten used to all that bickering, all that toy-throwing. She had even tried to convince her mom to let Eric come and live with them, but Eric's mom wouldn't let him even fly out to visit his dad.

Mya didn't know what to say, something that absolutely, positively never happened to her. Even when she was born, her mother said she came out of the womb mumbling and cooing. Yet there she was in the arms of Eric Baldini, who, for some odd reason, made her pulse quicken, and for a brief moment, seemed enormously sexy.

How odd.

"I…I need my shoes," she mumbled once he let go of their embrace.

He leaned over and her world spun a little as she watched him. Almost as if she'd just been passionately kissed. She took a step back and tripped over her own feet and fell down again, hard on the cement. Now her butt hurt and the fall caused her to bite her own lip. This falling thing was getting entirely too wacky.

When she looked up at him, the rain had completely stopped and the sun surrounded his body, making him appear almost angelic. She half expected to hear birds chirping and a choir singing, but instead a cop said, "There's no loitering. You'll have to move on."

Eric held out his hand. This time she took it. He held her shoes in his other hand. "We better get out of here before he has us towed away. You're bleeding." He touched her lip and a tingle shot through her. She sucked her bottom lip inside her mouth and tasted her own salty blood.

"Is it bad?" she asked looking into his eyes.

"No. It stopped." He smiled. Definitely less nerdy when he smiled. He'd actually grown up into a really handsome man.

Who knew?

"Where's your stuff?" he asked looking back toward the doors.

An absolute terror swept over her as she slipped her soaking wet shoes on her soaking wet feet. "You don't actually expect me to get in that thing with that crazed dog and that obnoxious smell do you? And just what is that smell, anyway?"

He opened his mouth.

She held up her hand. "Wait. I don't want to know. The dog is bad enough."

"Voodoo? He's a puppy dog once you get to know him."

The sun was beginning to dry her clothes, but she had to admit, she was still cold and getting very tired. All she wanted was to go home to Mom's.

"My mother actually sent you to pick me up?"

He nodded, grinning.

"My mother, who knows I have an unnatural fear of animals with teeth larger than mine, and hate dirt of any kind...that mother sent you?"

"Technically, my dad asked me, but he was calling on behalf of your mom."

So, they were both in on this little deal. Already they're trying to fix us up.

Mya thought about her options.

There weren't any.

Not really. She had no choice but to take a ride from a cute nerd, to whom she was strangely attracted, and had once thrown an entire box of crayons at, hitting him squarely in the head (she wondered if he remembered that). And who came with a man-eating bear of a dog inside a beat-up van.

It could be worse. It could still be raining.

WHEN ERIC'S DAD HAD PHONED HIM to pick up Mya, he pictured a completely different woman standing outside of baggage claim. He honestly believed she would be rather large. She'd been a chubby little girl who stuffed food in her mouth all day long, had short curly hair—Rita always seemed to cut Mya's hair in strange ultra-short styles—and weird glasses. Mya had worn glasses back then and whenever they'd fight, he would call her Four Eyes, of course.

But the girl in the floral dress with the strawberry hair down to her tiny waist, and a face that could bring the dead to life, wasn't exactly what he was prepared for. Nor was he prepared for her fear of dogs. Not that most grown men hadn't walked the other way when Voodoo was around, but her fear was borderline hysteria.

He opened the back of his van and tried to secure Voodoo in his cage, while Mya waited with her luggage on the sidewalk.

"This won't take but a minute," Eric told her, but the dog was ornery and wanted to give Mya a friendly welcome nudge. Mya stood as far away as she could. "He wants to say hello," Eric told her.

"Hi," she said, waving from her safe vantage point.

"I think he wants to smell you before you get in the van."

Mya's left eyebrow went up. He suddenly remembered how she could move each eyebrow independently. When they were about five or six, he thought she was an interplanetary alien because of it, but then he was a big fan of *Star Wars*.

"You can still do that."

"Do what?"

"That thing you do with your eyebrows." He tried to move his eyebrows independently, but couldn't.

"You remember that?"

"Yeah. It's not like it's a common thing."

"What else do you remember?"

"That you liked peas and spinach. What kind of kid likes peas and spinach?"

"You used to snitch butter out of the fridge and chew on your dad's vitamin E caps and make yummy sounds."

"I had a thing for oil."

It started to rain again, and she still wasn't in the van.

"You have to let him smell your hand or he's going to be restless the whole way."

"Aren't there enough smells in that van already? Why does he need mine?"

"Dogs like to know who's around them."

Mya slowly made her way up to the open door with her hand held out, but he could tell that she was ready to pull it back at any moment. He took hold of it, and she moved up closer. He liked the feel of her skin next to his.

Calm down. There's no hope here. She's way out of your league.

Voodoo stuck his nose up to their hands and took a couple long sniffs, but to Eric's surprise, Mya didn't pull back like he had expected. Instead, they stood there for an awkward moment holding hands...just like they did the day that he left when they were seven.

AFTER THE SMELL INTRODUCTION with Voodoo, a black pit-bull–bulldog mix with a head the size of a beach ball and teeth way too big to think about, and he was safely inside his black metal cage, Mya sprayed almost her entire bottle of Nanette Lepore around the foul-smelling van. Peach and cranberry permeated the air. Then, while Eric loaded her luggage right behind the front seats so Mya could keep track of it, she gingerly hoisted herself up into the passenger's seat. When everything and everyone was safely tucked inside, the trio was on their way home.

This ought to be good.

"You look so different," Eric said while he merged into the swarming traffic.

"Growing up will do that to you," Mya answered, not wanting to actually sit back in the faded gold cloth seat. She had no idea what kind of muck might be attached to it and didn't want whatever it was stuck to her bare back. She leaned slightly forward and held her obviously chewed seat belt out so it wouldn't touch her dress.

"No. I mean your hair's a different color, no glasses and you're, well, thin."

Mya turned to face him. "Are you saying I was fat? 'Cause I was never actually fat. I was simply big-boned."

"And you changed that?"

"I grew out of it."

"Oh." He stared at her for a moment, then back at the street, then back at her. "And your nose. I can remember you had a real—"

Okay, so Mya had had a nose alteration when she was nineteen. Nothing major. Just some tapering of the width and a little off the tip. It's not like she had her whole nose reconstructed or anything drastic. And so what if she *did* have a nose job. Was that some kind of crime or something?

"Shouldn't you be concentrating on your driving?" She forgot what she was doing and sat back in the chair, instantly feeling something sticky on her back. She leaned forward again.

Too late.

"Aw, what's on this seat?" she whined.

"Voodoo drools a little. It's the bulldog in him."

"He drools on your seats?"

"Only that one. It's where he usually sits."

Okay, I think I'm going to be sick.

She sneezed.

"Sorry, but the heater doesn't work. I've got a sweater in the back somewhere," Eric offered.

She could only imagine what a stinking, wet, hairy mess his sweater would be. The thought made her shiver out loud. "I don't really think I need it. Thanks."

They drove out of the airport in silence, while Voodoo literally snored like a mad bull in his cage. The mere sound of his raspy throat reminded her of those vicious teeth of his.

She sneezed again. Perhaps she was allergic to something inside the van. Oh, hell, she didn't even want to think about what it could be.

Once they were on the crowded freeway and headed to her mom's house, she decided the least she could do was make some polite conversation. After all, the man was giving her a ride home. "So, what about this weather?"

He chuckled. "We haven't seen each other since we were kids and that's the best you can do? You want to talk about the weather?"

All right, now he made her smile. "Okay. What are you into these days?" She thought she'd use some of her interviewing techniques.

"That's a start. I'm *into* a documentary. What about you?"

"I do trend analysis. In more familiar terms, I'm a trend spotter."

"Oh yeah? I heard about that. Seems like it would be a cool job."

So, he isn't so nerdy, after all.

"I like it. Matter of fact that's why—" And just as she was about to give him the skinny on her very important reason for being there, he suddenly got off the free-way miles from her mother's house.

"Tell me you know a shortcut, 'cause this isn't the best of neighborhoods to have something go wrong with this van of yours."

"Nothing's wrong. I just need to do some taping."

"Here? What could you possibly be taping here? A drug bust? A murder? What?"

"I'm working on my MFA in film."

"You're still in school?"

"Yeah. I graduate in June. I'm on spring break."

"This June. Like in three months?"

"Yeah. Cool, huh?"

"Yeah."

But Mya wasn't so sure it was cool. When he first told her he was working on a documentary she assumed it was for some big studio and it would be for something serious, like world peace and he might be up for an Oscar, and she could go to the awards in a Prada gown and get interviewed by Joan Rivers. Then she'd get discovered and land the starring role in the next Tom Cruise movie and they'd fall in love and…

But he's a film student!

He drove his van down side streets and straight into one of the more sketchy and bleak-looking areas of L.A. So maybe this was serious and she had misjudged him. Maybe he was doing something important about the downtrodden, the desperately poor and the hopeless in our society.

She looked at him with newfound respect. "What's your documentary about?"

"Bars."

Huh?

"Like in taverns?"

"Yeah."

"You're not serious."

Okay, don't judge. Maybe it's the decadence of the bars. Now that might be an angle.

"Why not? The saloons, taverns and bars of America made this country what we are today. They helped shape us. More historic events took place in saloons than any legal building in the whole of the U.S."

She stared at him, not quite sure she had heard him correctly. "You're not serious."

"You said that already."

"I'm assimilating the information." She turned to face him. "Let me get this straight, your premise is that saloons helped shape our country?"

"Damn straight. I'm heading up to Gold Country next. And a couple days ago I was in Tombstone. 'The town too tough to die.' I went to the Birdcage Theater where the prostitutes had their own rooms around the poker tables. Did you know that Wyatt Earp married a prostitute? He met her in that very saloon. How's that for tavern trivia?"

She was coming around. "Actually, that's kind of interesting. I didn't know that."

This could be good.

She thought she might get to the Oscars after all.

He stopped the van in front of a run-down tavern. Two bad-ass older guys, with lots of tattoos and gold chains, sat on the front stoop, giving them the look. You know, that look that said, "What the hell are you two doing here?"

Mya locked her door.

"Aren't you going to come in with me?"

"Where?"

"This is one of the oldest saloons in L.A. Just look at that architecture." He bent over to check out the view from the front window.

"You've got to be kidding."

"But Voodoo is going to need a walk, and I need to film this. Maybe you can walk him for me. Believe me, nobody will bother you with Voodoo."

"Voodoo will bother me." She wasn't stepping one foot out of the van. She had grown accustomed to the smell and wanted to stay right where she was, *thank you very much.*

"He gets upset when he has to go."

"Go where?"

"Piss. He needs to take a piss."

"And you expect me to walk him?"

"Yeah. If you would. Please."

He smiled over at her, but it was a fake smile. One of those pasted on things that used to drive her crazy when they were kids and he'd want to play soldier and she wanted to play anything but.

Voodoo started barking. Nothing too loud, only it had a guttural sound that made her nervous just being in the van with him. She didn't know what she was scared of most, Voodoo or the two guys on the stoop.

Eric continued to lure her as he jumped out with his handheld professional-looking camcorder. "I don't know if you should stay in there."

"Why?"

"Well, sometimes Voodoo—"

Suddenly the odor that she had gotten somewhat used to intensified.

"Ohmigod!"

She opened the door and leaped out of the van so fast the two guys sitting in front of the store stood up to watch. Eric filmed the whole thing.

Fine!

"What did you feed him? That's awful!" Mya hissed.

"Are you okay, lady?" one of the guys yelled from the stoop.

Mya turned and said, "Fine. I'm fine. Thanks." She pasted one of her own fake smiles on her face.

"Like I said, when he's gotta go, my boy's gotta go."

Mya followed Eric to the back of the van while he opened the doors. "Just get the dog out here, and don't take too long taping in there, 'cause I'm not going to last too long out here. This whole thing is insane."

"Great. I'll only be a couple minutes."

Eric freed Voodoo from his cage. The dog already wore a body harness with a thick black strap to hold him. He completely ignored Mya and jumped on the ground and headed for the nearest tree. The two scary guys slowly stood up and made their way into the tavern. A woman crossed the street as soon as she spotted the dog and a teenage boy hightailed it up the sidewalk.

Voodoo was like walking with a visible grenade. Everybody wanted to get out of your way.

So much for tattoos and mean looks.

"Here," Eric said, handing her the leash. "You better hold on with both hands. He's very strong."

Mya grabbed hold, wrapping the strap around one of her hands for extra strength. She figured as long as the creature didn't really look at her, she would be all right.

Eric went off happily taping the tavern, and even went inside, to apparently talk with the guys, while Mya held on to Voodoo.

Okay, she could do this. There was no reason to be scared of this animal. Eric had said he was a puppy dog, and he had done his smelling thing, so he was used to her scent.

Walking Voodoo didn't have quite the same feel as walking a schnauzer, or even a golden lab. Having Voodoo on the end of your leash was like walking a tiger. You went where he led you, and at the moment that meant a tiny patch of dirt in front of a scrawny stick of a tree a few yards away from the van.

As soon as he found his spot and marked it with his pee, he proceeded to take a dump. Mya looked away, wondering if there was a law in this neighborhood about cleaning up the mess. Of course, there was no way that she would even consider picking up whatever rot that dog emitted from his foul body.

Suddenly there was a tug on the leash. Mya turned to check him out and watched as Voodoo tried to cover his dump with his hind legs. He sent leaves, grass and his rotten whatever all over the place, with some of it landing on the parked pick-up truck next to him. And as if that wasn't enough, he lifted a leg and peed on the back tire.

"Oh, my God!" was all Mya could say as Voodoo ran from the crime scene with Mya in tow. He headed right back to the van. But there was somebody yelling at her and obviously chasing them from behind. Mya was not about to look back; besides, she could barely keep up with Voodoo's pace. But whoever was chasing them sounded very male, very big and enormously angry.

Eric suddenly appeared in front of the tavern, took one look at the situation and hurried to the back of his van. He opened one of the doors just as Voodoo leaped inside. Mya followed, tumbling in on top of him, then hitting the floor with a thud. There was something wet and yellow under Mya's hands. She desperately tried not to notice, but it was almost too much for her to assimilate. She told herself to relax, as long as it wasn't acid, she would be fine.

Eric closed the door, ran around to the front, jumped in and took off squealing as if they had just robbed that tavern and they were on the lam in some crazy movie.

Bonnie and Clyde and Voodoo.

When Mya looked up, Voodoo was staring right at her, obviously excited and waiting for a pat on the head for being such a good dog. She couldn't even think of touching him.

Then, as if he could hear her thoughts, he shook his head and saliva slapped her right in the face.

She sat up, wiped the spittle from her cheek and calmly proceeded to remove one of Eric's obviously expensive video cameras from its case. A very nice Panasonic DVCPRO Camcorder, to be precise.

This should get me home.

ERIC DROVE THE VAN while Mya scooted herself to the front. She knelt down behind him and said, in a matter-of-fact voice, "If you don't take me home right this minute, I'll throw your frickin' camera right out the frickin' window."

Eric glanced at her through his mirror. Sure enough she was holding his best camera up for ransom. It reminded him of when she threatened him with his boom box.

The girl still had spunk, he had to give her that.

"I know you're a little upset, but—"

"A little upset! I'm a whole lot upset and if I don't

get out of this stink-mobile pretty soon, there's no telling what I might do."

Eric remembered the time she had thrown his favorite Transformer down the toilet, then flushed and grinned at him as the water washed over their feet from the overflowing bowl. They were both grounded for an entire month, but Mya never seemed to care about the punishment once she was on a track of getting even.

Yeah, so maybe he *had* shaved Barbie's head bald, and maybe it *had* been her favorite doll, but he couldn't take all that incessant chattering all the time. The girl never shut up. Mya had been a vindictive child, but was she actually capable of throwing his camera out the window just because she wanted to go home? He gazed at her face once again through his mirror. She held the camera up next to the open passenger window.

Damn straight she was.

"All right. You win. I'll take you home, just put my camera down. Gently."

"How do I know you're telling the truth and you won't make another stop at an even worse tavern?"

"You have my word."

"And what's that good for these days?"

"Whatever you want. Dinner? A movie? My head on a platter."

"My mom's house is all I'm interested in at the moment. I'll take your head another time, thank you very much."

"We should be there in fifteen minutes, tops."

"Fine!"

Mya put his camera back in the case. Eric was somewhat relieved, but now he knew she still had that ornery streak. Part of him thought it was cute, but the other part of him thought he needed to watch his step. The girl could blow at any minute.

Eric watched as Mya stepped over the console and sank into the front seat. Her dress slid up her legs all the way to her red-and-white polka-dot panties and Eric flushed.

Don't get excited. She hates you right now.

"And could you please call off your dog," Mya said as Voodoo's head came poking through the center of the two seats.

"Down boy," Eric commanded. "Sit, you old dog, you."

Mya threw Eric a wry glance. Eric responded with a shrug.

"You guys are all alike," Mya said as she adjusted her dress around her fine legs.

"It's what we live for." He smiled at her, thinking that she'd see the humor, but she didn't smile back.

When Eric had volunteered to pick up Mya Strano from LAX, he'd never expected some hot-looking chick in a skimpy dress and legs that never quit. He also didn't expect her to be so East Coast. So with it. So New York. Oh, sure, he knew she'd been living in the Big Apple, working at some job her mother couldn't really describe, but he never imagined she would be a complete knockout. This whole trip back to L.A. could turn out to be very interesting.

Voodoo blew air through his closed lips, making a vibrating sound, and sighed. Eric reached back and patted him on the head.

WHEN THEY FINALLY PULLED UP in her mom's driveway, Mya couldn't say goodbye fast enough. "Well, I guess that's it, then," she told him, sticking out her hand for a not-so-friendly handshake. He took it, but as soon as he did, she slipped her hand out and turned to walk up the driveway.

There will be no hand-holding this time, buddy.

"Let me help you with your bags," he said as he pulled the handle up on the largest suitcase.

"No thanks," she insisted, almost ripping it out of his hand. She wanted to do everything herself from now on. She was home now and didn't need him for anything. Ever! "I've got it. It was so nice seeing you again. Maybe we'll run into each other again sometime...in the next twenty years."

She walked up the driveway hoping that he'd start his engine and drive away, but he didn't. She turned around and waved. Maybe he didn't get the hint. He always was a little slow at the uptake. "So, bye then. Have a safe trip up to Gold Country."

She turned around again. This time she headed straight for the side door, opened it with her key and pulled her suitcase inside. She turned one more time as she stood in the doorway and waved. But he just stood there, waving back, all full of smiles.

She closed the door, locked it and gave it a few pats as if that was her final statement on the subject.

"And to think for a moment there, I thought he was cute. Must have been temporary insanity."

Mya left everything by the kitchen door and walked into her mother's ridiculously large and totally upscale English Tudor house.

"Anybody here?" she yelled. "I'm home."

Home. There's no place like home.

It didn't matter that her mother wasn't there, nor

Grammy, nor Franko. What Mya really needed was a shower and a bed.

She made her way through the kitchen, decorated with walnut cabinetry and large Mexican tiles on the floor. Nothing had changed in the last ten years and Mya liked it that way. When she walked through the traditional dining room and up the wooden staircase to her old bedroom, she took comfort in knowing that no matter what went on in the outside world, her mother's house was always the same.

Mya gently knocked on her grandmother's bedroom door just to make sure she wasn't there. Grammy's hearing wasn't as good as it used to be, so Mya thought she'd give her another holler. But Grammy didn't answer.

Then she found her old room down at the end of the hall. It looked exactly like the day she'd left it, two years ago. She was absolutely thrilled to be in her own room.

Mya fell across her queen-size bed with its light green silk comforter. Absolute serenity overtook her as she spread out and enjoyed the luxury of not having that monster dog breathing in her ear. Her room smelled of lilacs and roses.

How marvelous.

Mya rolled herself up inside her comforter and fell asleep, or did she?

There was that damn bark again, only this time it came from somewhere inside the house.

3

MYA MUST HAVE JUMPED three feet off the bed when she heard that bark. At first she thought she'd dreamed it, but when she heard it again, she knew the animal was close by. Which meant, of course, that Eric was somewhere close by. Was there no rest for the weary? No port in the storm? No time to recover? She rolled over and pulled the blankets up over her head.

"Honey, I thought you'd never wake up," Rita Strano announced. She sat on the bed next to Mya and put her hand on her daughter's shoulder. Mya rolled over and stared up at her mother's always beautiful face.

Her mother's eyes widened and an eyebrow shot up. "What the heck happened? Are you all right?"

A shot of adrenaline raced through Mya's veins. "What do you mean?"

"Do you feel okay? You look rather...awful." Her mother took in a sharp breath. "Were you in an accident?"

Mya yawned and stretched. Her jaw ached and her right hip hurt. How odd, she thought. "Define *accident*."

"Don't kid. Do you hurt anywhere? You look like something the dog dragged in."

Mya smiled. Her bottom lip stung. "He did." She was beginning to get somewhat worried over all the aches and pains.

"I don't understand," Rita grumbled, shaking her head.

Mya scooted out of bed thinking she needed to get a good look at herself in her bathroom mirror. She didn't remember being in an actual accident, but then she'd read that if the accident's really bad, a person can't remember it. Like your brain saves you from the trauma or something. Okay, but she didn't have any deep pain anywhere. Not really. Her lip hurt, and her hip was sore, and her ankle was a little stiff, and maybe her jaw felt a little weird, but nothing major. No headache. No nausea. No acid indigestion…no wait, she never got that. What was her mother talking about?

When Mya glanced in the mirror, she had no choice but to let out a short burst of a scream at the woman staring back at her.

Her mother came running in. "What's the matter?"

Not only was Mya's hair full of dried dog saliva and some kind of unrecognizable yellow substance, but her right cheek was slightly bruised, her bottom lip was swollen and her pretty floral dress was torn and just plain filthy.

"This is all your fault, Mom. You sent that…that disaster-on-wheels to pick me up from the airport. Are you trying to punish me for something?" Mya examined her bruised cheek and swollen lip in the mirror. She couldn't believe there could be so much damage from one little fall. All right, maybe two falls. Then she remembered jumping into the back of the van, and the creepy yellow stuff, and how she had hit her face on the camera case.

"Of course not. I sent a comfy black limo to fetch you." She hesitated for a moment. "Or did I tell Franko to order the limo?" She paused and thought for a second. "Yes. That was it. I got really busy with a Spanish blackberry torte and asked Franko to send over the limo. Oh, my! Did something go wrong with the limo driver? Did he attack you? You can't trust anybody these days."

"I *wish* the limo driver had attacked me. At least I would've been inside a clean car rather than a vile, stinking hell-on-wheels. It was Eric."

"Eric attacked you?" She sat down on the closed toilet seat. "Who knew? And he was such a nice little boy. It's that devil mother of his. I always knew she was a bad influence on that boy. We'll send him to jail for the rest of his miserable life."

Her mother was spinning out of control. Mya had to put a stop to it, or the police would be raiding Eric's van at any moment…which, considering all he had put her through, might not be a bad idea. "Mom. Everything's fine. Relax. It was nothing like that. Eric never touched me, well, except for a hug, which was way too long, by the way."

She abruptly stopped staring at herself in the mirror. The yellow stuff was like glue in her hair and she had to get it out of there. "I have to take a shower this instant or I'll explode."

"That's my girl. You need a good outlook on all of this. We'll work it out, later, at dinner. I'm sure whatever happened between you two can be resolved."

"Does this mean he's coming to dinner?"

"Of course he is. He's like a son to me."

"A minute ago you were ready to put him in jail."

"But now I'm not. See, it's already working out."

Mya pulled her dress up over her head and threw it on the white tile floor. Her mother picked it up. "Should I keep this as evidence, or should I burn it?"

Thoughts of a trial with Eric and her stained dress swirled around in Mya's head. A long trial, with Calista Flockhart as her lawyer, and Lucy Liu as the judge. They'd fine him for a million dollars for causing Mya so much stress, but Eric wouldn't be able to pay. She'd end up with his van. And Voodoo!

"Burn it!" she ordered. "Leave no thread uncharred."

"I'll get right to it. Enjoy your shower, sweetheart."

Her mom left while holding the dress out in front of her with one hand. Mya closed the bathroom door, opened the glass door on the shower, turned on the water so it was nice and hot, stripped off her underwear and stepped under the gentle spray.

She wanted to stand there for the next hundred years and let the warm water run over her aching body. She had little aches and pains everywhere. She wondered how a simple ride from the airport could have caused all of this. She even had a bruise on her left shin.

Next time she'd take a cab or rent a car or steal a skateboard. She figured her lack of transportation judgment must have something to do with the coming-home thing. That unconscious need to be taken care of. The desire to return to the child stage, or some such madness. Why else would she have agreed to hitch a ride from Eric Baldini? The Tormentor.

Then she thought of how incredibly sexy she had felt when Eric had stared at her legs. She hadn't been that turned on over something that simple in, well, forever.

He had the best eyes, an olive-green color, and could probably be astonishingly attractive if he just dressed the part. Maybe a little product in his hair to make it stand up a little, a classic Calvin Klein shirt, and some H&M slacks. And where did he get those absolutely horrid blue shoes?

But why was she even thinking about Eric? He and his monster dog lived in Georgia for heaven's sake. It was like swooning over somebody who lived in Brooklyn.

He may as well live on another planet!

She told herself to stop daydreaming and to think about her purpose for coming to L.A. in the first place. To save *La Dolce Rita*.

She needed to focus.

Now that she was safely home, she would go over her notes and present them at dinner. Turning, she let the water run down her face and belly while she lathered her hair, carefully. She turned again, rinsed and lathered it three more times, just to make extra sure the yellow goo was completely gone, along with any Eric Baldini residue.

Okay, she was back on track. Back in control.

Mya finished washing, dried off, dressed in a white Hugo Boss shirt and Ralph Lauren pink capris while she mentally prepared her speech on *rules for cool*. She wanted to wow Franko and her mom with her plan, and by tomorrow when the actual meeting rolled around, everyone would be prepared for the perfect pitch, Mya-style.

ERIC HAD WAITED PATIENTLY for someone to come home to let him in after Mya had locked him out. It wasn't a long wait, maybe an hour or so. Obviously, no one had told Mya that he was her mother's house guest for the next two weeks while his dad's house was being renovated. He wondered how Mya would react to his constant presence after their afternoon together. Not that it was a necessarily bad afternoon. It was more in the somewhat strained category of afternoons.

At one point, he actually toyed with the idea of getting a room somewhere, but then decided against it because of his dog. Voodoo was a point of contention to most hotel and motel owners. It was just easier to sleep on a mat in the van while he traveled. However, sometimes getting a shower was something of a problem, but he hadn't expected to have to pick up Mya at the airport the very day he arrived in L.A. That was his father's idea, and not a very bright one. He never should have agreed to it, but his dad always could get him to do things he didn't want to do.

Now, as he stood in front of the bathroom mirror off the guest room, shaving off his three-day-old beard, he wondered if giving her a ride home had been a smart move. The look on her face when he hugged her said it all. The woman wanted to run, not hug. He could see it in her eyes, those fantastic smoky eyes. And that body.

He put on his only clean T-shirt, black, and a pair of shiny blue knee-length shorts. Admittedly, he didn't look quite up to her funky standards, but at least he didn't smell anymore. He blamed the obnoxious odor on those bottles of spicy Cajun mustard his father had forced him to lug back from New Orleans. Voodoo couldn't leave anything alone once it was inside the van.

Of course, Eric should have cleaned it up before he picked up Mya, but Voodoo had just ripped open the plastic bottles on the way and there hadn't been any time.

This whole thing had been his father's idea. Eric was happily filming his saloons when his dad had called him, begging for some help with *La Dolce Rita*. Not that Eric had a single idea of what to do to help, but his dad insisted that he come out anyway. He never could say no to his dad. The man had a way of making everything sound exciting. Like it was Eric's idea. And this was no exception. By the time he drove into L.A. he was feeling euphoric about the possibilities, even though he still hadn't one single clue of what to do to help. When he had heard that Mya was on her way out as well, he'd hoped they could work together on the show, but after everything that had happened that afternoon, he was sure the show was categorically doomed.

"Ah, that's my beautiful Mya," Rita said crisply as Mya walked into the kitchen. Rita held out her arms and Mya embraced her mother. "Do you feel better, sweetheart?"

"Much," Mya answered while they hugged even tighter.

Rita was the kind of mom every girl dreamed of, loving, beautiful and totally her own woman. It had always been just Mya and her mom. Her dad had died soon after she was born, so Mya hadn't ever known her real father, just Franko. Rita owned several small businesses and some prime real estate, ran their house and looked amazingly young for her fifty-three years. She just needed a little boost to that incredible look of hers.

Franko had his back to her, stirring something in the corner of the kitchen. He wore a large white apron over his casual clothes, just like Emeril. Actually, Franko looked a little like Emeril, with his stocky build and black, perfectly combed hair. But Franko had a gorgeous smile, no doubt where Eric got his smile from, that he was quick to share for almost any reason. Franko was one of those content, happy men who never seemed to worry about anything.

"Ciao, bella," he said as he turned to face Mya, his hands in the air, beaming as if he were truly surprised to see her. Franko had come over from Italy when he was just nineteen and never really lost his fabulous accent. Thus the reason he and Rita had been so successful. She was his American voice.

Mya was surprised at her reaction to seeing him. A thrill raced over her. Franko had virtually raised her as his own daughter, and Mya loved him for it. The only thing that kept her from calling him Dad was a lack of a marriage certificate between him and her mom.

"Ciao, bello," Mya echoed and held out her arms as well. She loved to be hugged by Franko. He made her feel safe and warm and he smelled of anisette, one of her favorite liqueurs.

"You look'a like the queen," he announced while they embraced.

"The queen of what?" Mya asked as she pulled away from him and gazed into his smiling face. She loved his rugged Italian face, full of love and compassion, and excitement. He had a dimple in each cheek, and a broad forehead and sparkling almond eyes.

"The queen of'a my heart."

She melted back into his embrace for a few seconds longer. "What more could a girl want?"

"A FANCY DINNER DRESS," Grammy Strano repeated as she scooped a few more clams into her dish. The two families had gathered around Rita's long dinner table, and Grammy was busy giving a lecture on dinner etiquette. She still wore her golden hair in a stylish page-boy, and wore pink cat-eye glasses with rhinestones embedded in the corners. She kept her weight just under slim, had silky, olive-colored skin and a smile that was contagious. "In my day, the women came to the dinner table dressed in gowns and the men wore suits. None of this shorts business."

She sat next to Eric and gazed down at his legs, scolding him with her eyes. Then she addressed the rest of the group around the table. Grammy liked being the center of attention, and always spoke her mind. "Dinner was an event. Then after dinner somebody would sing or play an instrument."

"I can play chopsticks on the piano," Eric announced.

"Great! Why don't you play it for us after dinner," Grammy urged, as she tucked a lace hankie down the front of her silver gown. She wore one of the many dresses she had designed for various movie stars during the forties and fifties. Lucille Marie Nudi had been one of the top fashion designers in Hollywood. She still clung to the notion that a woman needed to wear a hat and gloves every time she left the house and, apparently, a ball gown at dinner.

"Ma, we don't have a piano," Rita offered.

"Why not? With all your money, you'd think you

could buy this boy a stinking piano so we could have some entertainment once in awhile."

Mya tried to make Grammy understand the situation. The poor woman was obviously losing her memory. "Eric lives in Georgia, Gram."

"I know that," she said curtly, then turned to Eric and asked, "Did you bring your piano?"

"No, but I brought my dog."

The dog from hell.

"Does he do any tricks?"

Let me tell you about the little trick he did in front of a truck today.

"He can twirl a basketball on his nose."

Mya sat back to listen. This was getting good.

"That'll do. Now I can eat knowing that after dinner we have entertainment. I've got a nice suit upstairs in my office that I designed for Clark Gable. You can wear that."

"It would be my honor," Eric said, giving a little bow. If you wanted to win Grammy's approval, all anybody had to do was agree with her outrageous ideas. Eric seemed to know just what it took, because Grammy beamed from ear to ear.

All of this sucking up was temporary and he would be leaving right after the dog show.

The dinner table was covered from one side to the other with plates of enticing food. Both Rita and Franko had outdone themselves with culinary treats: pasta with clams, cockles and mussels in a wine, garlic and butter sauce; a sweet-pepper and leek tart; penne with broccoli, anchovies and raisins; homemade focaccia with tomatoes and fresh basil; roasted leg of lamb stuffed with artichokes; a zucchini flan and several bottles of Italian red and white wines.

"I've got some fantastic ideas of how to recreate the show," Mya announced during a break in the conversation. "I was thinking of a more colorful set. Something along the lines of what's happening in modern Italy. You need to appeal to a younger audience. The nineteen to thirty-five group. We might even do some shows to target teens. We need to sparkle to appeal to the 'now generation.' Maybe add some reds and oranges to the set to go with the kinds of food that are easy, healthy and visually exciting. I think you need to cook some exciting entrées with more panache, more flair for the daring.

"And, Mom, I've planned a makeover for you. Nothing drastic, just a little younger look. You too, Franko. It's time to get rid of your white apron for simple slacks and a printed shirt. Maybe some sideburns and product in your hair to give it that edge everyone seems to be after."

Everyone fell silent at the table.

Probably too excited to speak.

She knew she had totally captivated them with her incredibly savvy ideas. That it wouldn't take long for them to actually stand up and applaud or throw flowers…or maybe not.

"Maybe this is good. I don't know, but we should hear what my Eric, he has to say," Franko added.

"Eric?" Mya said, completely thrown off course.

"Yes, dear," Rita said. "Eric is going to help you. Won't it be nice with you two working together again? Just like when you were kids. I think it's a heavenly idea. Don't you, dear?" Rita waited for Mya to answer. Franko waited for Mya to answer. Grammy waited. Even Eric waited for an answer.

And during that moment of anticipation, Voodoo barked and something crashed in the kitchen.

At least that dog was good for something.

4

"THIS DOG, HE HAS the good taste," Franko announced as everyone watched Voodoo consume the last bites of what had to be a perfect peach-and-raspberry tart.

My absolute favorite dessert.

The beast had no shame. He looked up at the group as they huddled in the kitchen doorway and he belched out his total satisfaction, then shook his head. Voodoo had managed to pull the tart down from the counter, and with two bites had devoured the entire pastry delight.

"That dog needs to be kept outside, locked in a cage, inside Eric's van, on his way to Gold Country," Mya snarled.

"Don't be silly. He's our houseguest," Rita explained in that sweet lilt of a voice she got whenever she wasn't quite sure of how to respond to a taxing situation.

"Sorry 'bout that," Eric said as he made his way over to Voodoo. "I thought I tied him up tight, but I guess he got loose somehow."

"The poor little thing must have been hungry," Grammy added. "You need to feed him. How can you expect your puppy to do doggie tricks on an empty stomach?"

Mya pulled her mother back into the dining room to

clarify a few things. "What do you mean he's *our house-guest?* Isn't that *dinner guest?*"

"Well, not exactly. Franko's house is being remodeled and he's been staying here, so it's only natural that Eric and his little friend stay here too. Besides, if you and he are going to work together, this will be much easier. Don't you think?" Rita stood in front of her daughter, smiling, as if this was all perfectly acceptable to Mya. But for Mya this was all perfectly unacceptable.

"Mom, what can you be thinking? Why would I want to do anything with Eric? You know how that boy infuriates me."

"Man."

"What?"

"You called Eric a boy. He's a grown man now. Just as you like to be referred to as a grown woman. I'm sure he likes the same courtesy."

Mya was losing all patience now. In less than five hours her mother had managed to cause her to wish she were back in New York City fighting overcrowded subways.

Or Vegas.

She could be in Vegas right now interviewing teens at the Forum inside Caesar's Palace. *At least Grace would be happy.*

"Mom, you know Eric and I never got along." She was going for logic now. Something her mother was good at accepting.

"That's not true. What about the time I caught you two out by the shed? You seemed to be getting along just fine then."

So logic wasn't the answer.

"That was child abuse." Mya had always hoped that

her mother didn't remember that scene. Besides, nothing really happened but a little touchy-feely stuff...and maybe a peek down his pants. And she let him peek down her pants, but it couldn't have been for more than a second.

What can you see in a second?

"Don't be silly. It can't be child abuse if you're both children."

"He was a pervert."

Rita tapped her index finger on her top lip. Always a sign that she was thinking, and her mom had a crisp, sharp memory. "I seem to remember *you* looking down *his* pants and reaching—"

"I never reached for anything!"

"Whatever you say, dear."

"I can't do this. I have to go to Vegas. My job depends on it."

"If that's what you have to do, then that's what you have to do. I wouldn't want you to lose your job because of me."

A tear rolled down her mother's check.

Mya's anger immediately vanished and guilt took hold. "Mom, please don't cry. I don't really have to go to Vegas. Yet. It can wait until after the meeting tomorrow."

"Thank you, sweetheart. I don't know what I would have done without you."

"It'll be all settled tomorrow."

"Of course it will, dear," Rita sniffled. "I have complete faith in you...and Eric, of course."

"Of course," Mya said crisply, trying desperately to hide her anger over Eric's unwanted and unneeded help.

The two women hugged as Grammy, Eric and Voo-doo walked by them. "Turn off the waterworks, Rita, the entertainment's about to begin," Grammy gleefully said. She and Eric walked by arm in arm. Grammy in her ball gown and Eric in a Clark Gable suit.

If it weren't for the fact that Mya was steaming mad at the whole situation, she might have commented on how absolutely gorgeous Eric looked, but under the circumstances, she merely smiled at both him and her grandmother as they strolled by.

Rita smiled at her daughter and whispered, "All I ask is if the two of you want to compare body parts, this time would you please go someplace where I won't find you."

"That will *never* happen," she snarled in a clear, loud voice.

Rita leaned in closer. "Never say *never*, dear. It's a sure sign that you've been thinking about doing it." She winked at Mya and followed Grammy to the living room.

ERIC WAS DISAPPOINTED when Mya didn't show up for the "after-dinner entertainment." Voodoo was on his best behavior, actually able to balance not only a bas-ketball, but an orange, a grapefruit and a bowl of ice cream, all of which he ate…well, everything except for the basketball, of course.

When it was all over and Eric had returned the Clark Gable suit, which made him look incredibly dapper, ac-cording to Grammy, he made a beeline for the whirlpool bathtub he'd spotted earlier in the bathroom off his bedroom. While the water filled the tub, he threw in whatever salts and oils he could find on the shelves next to the mirror. They instantly started a billow of bubbles. He couldn't wait to step into the hot bubbly water. It was the one thing he remembered most about visiting Rita's house. He would play for hours in the bathtub with all his toys, and sometimes Mya would even join him. The concept of an adult Mya naked in his bathtub sent a jolt of excitement to his groin.

Down boy.

He walked out of the bathroom and into his bedroom to wait for the tub to fill up and to get his iPod mini so he could listen to some music while he soaked.

MYA WANTED NOTHING MORE than to take a long hot bath, which to her amazement, someone, probably her mother, had started for her in the adjoining bathroom. Her mom had actually added all the right salts and bubbles to the water and the temperature was just right. What a sweet mom she had. Always thinking about her daughter's needs. It was times like these that Mya appreciated her mother's attentiveness, her always knowing just what Mya needed, her thoughtfulness.

The absolute sweetest mom in the entire world.

Mya couldn't get out of her clothes fast enough.

And just as she was completely naked, leaning over the massive tub to test the water, who should show up from the other door, wearing nothing but a grin? Eric Baldini.

Mya leaped into the water, screaming out her surprise as she sank into the bubbles.

Eric grabbed the nearest towel, which happened to be a face cloth, a tiny face cloth, and covered his…well, let's just say that things had grown since the shed incident.

"What are you doing here?" Mya snarled, as she covered her breasts in bubbles.

"What am *I* doing here? What are you doing in *my* tub?"

"I believe this is my mother's house and therefore, this would be *my* tub!"

"So that gives you the right to just commandeer my bath water?"

"Clearly, my mom started this bath for me. Besides, this room is off my old bedroom."

"It also adjoins mine. Your mom had nothing to do with it. It's my bath, so if you don't mind…"

He made a gesture as if he expected her to get out. She couldn't believe his arrogance. His audacity. His really amazing body, with those muscular shoulders, and that incredible chest…

He must spend hours in the gym. And those thighs!

"You can't be serious?" Mya grumbled.

"Why wouldn't I be?"

Mya looked around for a towel and realized that she hadn't even thought to get one when she first stripped, and now the closest towel was way over on the other side of the room, hanging neatly from a chrome hook.

"Because you can't really expect me to just walk… I'm not getting out. You'll have to wait until I'm through."

"Have it your way," he said as he dropped his penis shield and stepped into the water.

"You can't do this," she hissed as his legs slid up next to hers. A strong shiver of excitement ran up her body. She wanted to be angry, and push him away or run, but he politely moved his legs out of the way so that they barely touched her.

"Why not? You used to slip into my bathtub when we were kids. It's payback time." He snickered and it instantly brought back memories of how he used to be when she would jump into his bath water just to torment him, and steal his toys. Of course, they were all of five at the time.

"That was different."

"How?"

"Our parts were smaller."

"You noticed?" He leaned back in the tub, making himself comfortable. She half expected him to close his eyes and take a nap.

"Oh, and like you didn't."

"I had no choice. You were standing right in front of me."

"A gentleman would have turned the other way." She scooped up some of the bubbles to better hide herself.

"I may have claimed to be a lot of things, but a gentleman was never on the list."

He smirked while his foot slid up against her right hip.

"If we're going to stay in this tub together, which it looks like we are, would you please refrain from touching me."

He moved his leg away from her. "I'll try, but I have to admit, I like your new body parts much better than the old ones. Are you sure you don't want to do a little anatomy study for old times' sake?"

"As tempting as that might be, I think we should just stick to sharing a bath."

Although, the vision of a wet, sudsy interlude did sound rather alluring to her at the moment.

No. She didn't need to have sex with another street-vendor type. If she was going to have sex with somebody, she wanted it to be with a guy she was actually thinking of starting up an honest-to-God relationship with, and not just some hot, slippery, sensuous, muscle-bound, glorious-when-wet type.

She reached over and turned on the cold-water spigot in the middle of the tub, probably exposing her breasts, and touching his feet as she moved, but she couldn't stand the heat. Then she sat back again while the cold water mixed with the hot.

"Um. That was nice. Could you do that again, please?" he mused as he rolled his head on the back of the tub to get a better angle for the peep show.

Then, for some reason, probably because she was borderline crazy with random sex cravings and needed to calm down, she remembered what had happened at dinner, and she instantly cooled off…causing her to lean forward again to turn off the running water. However, this time, she made sure her bubble-bra was in place.

"Tell you what," he mumbled with that pre-sex voice guys tend to get when they're trying to lure a woman into their bed. "I'll show you mine, if you show me yours."

She squinted, trying to get an angle on all of this bathtub wooing. Then she came up with a brilliant idea…of course. And Mya considered herself the queen of brilliant ideas. The star of knowing what would work and what wouldn't. What captured the mind of the masses, middle America, the world and the occasional pervert.

"Okay…but there have to be a couple rules."

"Whatever you want." He sat up. Bubbles slid down his fabulous chest.

"Great. You have to agree not to interfere with any of my ideas for *La Dolce Rita.*"

"Scout's honor." He did the three-finger thing.

"You were a Boy Scout?"

"Only for three months until my mother started to date my troop leader. It got too embarrassing after that."

"I don't want to know."

"I don't want to tell you."

"All right, then. And just like when we were five, there's no touching in this game."

"Where's the fun in that?" His hand splashed down into the water.

"Who said anything about fun? This is strictly a business deal." She slid up straighter, just to give him a peek at her fabulous, size 34-C, completely natural full breasts. I mean, why not lure the guy in while you've got him dangling on the line?

Men are so easy.

"Is that the only thing you can think of—business?"

"We don't have time for anything else. You have a documentary to film, and I have a show to save."

"But…"

"Take it or leave it. I can get out right now, and cover every inch of me with bubbles, or we can play peep show. It's your choice."

She began scooping up mounds of bubbles to cover herself.

"Okay, I agree, but we stand facing each other for a full five minutes."

"Never going to happen. That's way too long."

"Okay, a full minute, but there's no talking."

"Why?"

"Too distracting."

"We don't have a timer."

"I'll count."

"No. I'll count."

"We'll both count."

"On three we stand." Mya's heart was pounding in her chest. The whole idea of this excited her more than, well, more than she could ever remember. She really didn't know if she could stand in front of him for that long. It somehow seemed like an eternity.

"How 'bout half a minute?"

"You've already agreed."

Mya took a deep breath to calm herself. It didn't work. She could feel herself losing control of her limbs, perhaps even her mind.

He said, "On three, then."

"On three."

"One," they said in unison as she sighed, heavily.

"Two." He took hold of one side of the tub and brought his legs in tight to stand.

She did the same. Her heart was in her throat.

"Three…"

"…4…5…6…"

The suds slipped down her body causing a cascade of flashes of silky skin to peek through. The scent of the bath salts wafted up and surrounded him, coconut and vanilla, like a rich, creamy cake. He liked the roundness of her. God, she was even hotter than he had imagined.

"…15…16…17…"

He had a chest any girl would swoon over, tight, hairless with each muscle well defined. His shoulders were strong as if Michelangelo himself had designed them. And his stomach, well, there wasn't one, just more muscle that led down to…

"…24…25…26…"

There was a dim light in the room so Eric couldn't see her as well as he would have liked. He wanted to reach across and hold her in his arms, feel her pressed up against him, naked, but she had that look on her face that told him to keep his distance. If she was still the girl he'd known when they were five, he knew better than to cross her. Anything could happen.

"…37…38…39…"

The suds had inconveniently collected around his penis, but she could tell he had definitely matured into a man. At five or six, the tiny thing hadn't looked very promising, not that she had thought about it at the time, but her memories were quite vivid, despite what she had confessed to her mother.

"…45…46…47…"

The suds dropped from her incredibly full, round breasts. Her beautiful pink nipples standing taut, her stomach flat and her hips round and inviting. He was dying now, trying to stay calm, but he could feel the blood surge. He was grateful for the suds.

"…54…55…56…"

Mya could barely stand, she was so hot for him, and he for her, from what she could tell. Her knees were shaking and her stomach trembled. She was sure he could see it. She told herself this torture was almost over, but God, how she wanted him. If he had taken one step forward, moved one inch in her direction, it would be all over. No way would they make it out of that tub without sex. Hot, steamy sex.

"…57…58…59…"

All he wanted was a simple smile, something, anything and he would take her without even thinking. That was it, he couldn't think. Not now. Not with the crazy state he was in.

"…60…"

But neither one of them moved…until Rita walked in.

5

OKAY, SO THE BATHTUB ACTION had been amazingly naughty, and if it hadn't been for Rita walking in somewhere way past the minute mark, Mya and Eric probably would have done it, right there in the bubbles. *Wouldn't that have been amazing?*

But it hadn't happened. Instead, her mother screamed and that had ended the moment.

Why her mother had walked in was still a mystery to Mya when the woman had her own bathroom down at the other end of the hall, but Mya was grateful for the interruption...not really, but she forced herself into thinking she was.

She really didn't want to dwell on what could have been, and she *really, really* didn't want to talk about it with her mother, considering the woman's timing was almost uncanny.

The thing about it was, Mya hadn't slept very well last night and all she could think of this morning was Eric. It was enough to make a girl lose her focus. Her mission. Her cool.

Plus, she found it odd that she actually had some kind of emotional attraction to Eric. Some kind of need to be around him.

She thought it was all too distracting. After all, she

hadn't seen the guy in like forever, and hadn't even thought about him in decades. All right, so maybe that wasn't exactly true. She'd thought about him a lot, but who wouldn't? He was her first love. Didn't all little girls dream about their first love? She told herself it was a completely natural phenomenon of growing up, and nothing to get too upset over. She'd never see him again after this whole competition was over so why stress over something that could never be?

You grow up and move on. Simple. Easy. *La, la, la. No stress.*

"Are you all set for the meeting, dear?" Mya jumped at the sound of Rita's voice.

"Mom. Don't do that!"

"Do what, sweetheart?"

"Scare me like that?"

"I don't see how I can scare you when I've been sitting here for the last hour."

She had a point.

The two women sat at a round glass table out on the patio and shared a pitcher of iced tea and a tray of assorted homemade yummy Franko-pastries and sliced fruit. Her mom didn't seem to want to cook breakfast anymore because she was trying to keep her "girlish figure." Not that she ever had one. Rita was always a little plump—pleasantly plump, of course.

They sat in front of a massive backyard pool that had been recently resurfaced with blue Italian tiles. The tiles made the entire pool seem luminous in the sunshine, and had taken months to install, according to her mom, but well worth it. Her mom liked to keep up with what was happening in the neighborhood, and according to the latest trend, if you didn't have your pool redone with Italian blue glass, you simply didn't belong.

Of course, her mother never actually used the pool. She couldn't swim.

A white umbrella shaded the two women from the morning sun and kept the sparkling tiles from glistening in their eyes.

"You're right. It's just me. Sorry, Mom."

Mya fidgeted in her seat, tapped her foot, then shook her leg. Her concentration was completely gone. She sat up straight. Placed her feet firmly on the ground and sighed.

Perhaps all the twitching had something to do with the four glasses of tea she had just consumed.

Or did all these involuntary bodily movements have more to do with Eric?

Oh, hell. Not Eric.

Silence. Her heart pounded in her throat, just like it had the previous night while standing in the tub.

Her mother grinned over at her. Mya returned the gesture, wondering if mothers in fact could actually hear their daughters' thoughts. The notion made her cringe, but it would account for that sixth sense her mom always seemed to have. What other reason could there be for mothers walking in at the most inappropriate moments? There had to be some mental mother/daughter telepathy going on or else the whole thing was just too freaky.

Her mom took a sip of tea and relaxed in her chair. Mya's attention returned to the e-mail she was writing to Grace.

It was the perfect California day. The sun was shining, a soft breeze whistled through the palm trees, and birds chirped happy little tunes while news choppers circled overhead. All was right with the world.

Rita slowly leaned in and whispered, "Would it be okay to ask you a question, or am I scaring you again?"

Mya gazed over at her mom. She was radiant this morning in her soft-pink tailored dress and matching shoes. Her hair was piled high in a conservative bun, and she wore a white gardenia just behind her left ear. Her mom's makeup was flawless, and her smile, perfection. She was a strikingly beautiful woman, who required a complete makeover if this was ever going to work.

"No. You're not scaring me. Ask away."

"Are you ready for the meeting?"

Part of Mya's attention went back to her computer screen and she sent the e-mail to Grace, then she quickly checked on Youth Smarts' Web site to learn that a chess-boxing club had opened in Berlin—two minutes of boxing and four minutes of chess. It was a mental/physical kind of "sport" that seemed to be the latest craze. She made a note to herself to check it out later. It might be something that she could pitch to Blues Rock Bistro.

"Absolutely. Your producers are going to be blown completely away with my ideas. I have an amazing presentation, and I even contacted the Side Room and they'd love to do your music. They're the hottest new sound in L.A."

"They're not those hip-hop people, are they? 'Cause I don't think I understand that kind of music."

Mya finished off her fifth glass of tea and said, "Mom, I know you. These guys are more of a cross between early Beatles and a young Michael Jackson.

They're totally cool. You and Franko are going to love them."

Mya's laptop buzzed with last minute e-mails. Her boss, Grace, was getting antsy about Blues Rock Bistro and wanted to know what kind of progress, if any, she'd made with their new look. Unfortunately, Mya hadn't had time to actually do anything…well, except for that chess-boxing thing. And the more she thought about it, the more she knew that Blues Rock Bistro could do something similar, but she wasn't sure how that would work yet.

Anyway, she'd written back that she had their presentation completely under control and was working out a terrific plan.

Okay, so she had stretched the truth, a little. It was for Grace's own good. The woman would have a coronary if she knew what was really going on. *Absolutely nothing.* And Mya didn't want Grace's health hanging over her head. Besides, once the meeting with the producers was over, Mya was confident that she would have plenty of time for actual work.

She sighed and stretched out her legs under the table.

Mya hadn't seen Eric or his miserable beast of a dog since last night, and she was grateful for the lack of contact. He and Franko had gone off early in the morning on some kind of errand. Perhaps she wouldn't actually see him all day. That was fine with her. She'd immerse herself in her work, then at dinner, she'd consider talking to him, but it would only be to tell him his new duties. He'd become her slave of sorts, and she, his master.

The thought made her smile. *He could wear one of those skimpy Roman toga things, and she'd wear a sheer…*

"I don't mean to disturb you when you're working, but shouldn't we be going, dear? It takes about an hour to get to the studio," Rita warned, right in the middle of a perfectly wonderful fantasy. "Our driver is probably already here." Her mom didn't like to drive herself to studio meetings. She wanted to arrive calm and refreshed, not stressed from fighting with traffic.

"The meeting isn't until three. We have plenty of time," Mya answered with an actual lilt to her voice. She'd turned a corner in the world of nerves, and had regained her self-confidence.

"Eric wanted it earlier because Voodoo has an ear problem and needed to go to the vet. Poor darling. So I changed it to noon."

"Eric! No. Not Eric. We made a pact last night. He has nothing to do with this anymore. He doesn't need to go to the meeting. Please change it back to three, Mom. I'm not ready for a meeting at noon."

"I can't change it again, dear. They'll think I'm nutty. I think we should leave or we're going to be late."

"But, I'm not dressed for a meeting." Hell, she was barely dressed for sitting out by the pool. Mya wore striped green, gray, aqua and white Ann Klein shorts and a green sleeveless T. She had planned on wearing her brown Kenneth Cole power suit to the meeting, but it still needed pressing.

She stood up, and the world spun for a moment. Now she was doubly nervous, if that was even possible. She was the one who would be having the coronary, not Grace.

"This is California, Mya. You look perfect." Rita stared at Mya for a moment. "But you might want to change your shirt. Drama Queen may not be the appropriate phrase to hit them with if you want to make a good impression."

"When do we *have* to leave?"

Her mom glanced at her platinum wristwatch, a gift from Franko just last Christmas. "You have about eight minutes."

Mya shut down her laptop, shoved it into its case, grabbed all her papers and rushed into the house.

Grammy met her at the door. "I have the perfect thing for you to wear. Katharine Hepburn was supposed to wear it in *Desk Set*." She paused. "Or was it *Woman of the Year*? I can't remember, but it was magical on her. I took it out this morning just in case."

"Thanks, Gram, but I don't have time to—"

"I'm telling you, this suit is magical." Grammy stood in front of Mya, smiling, pleading with her eyes. Mya knew how much Grammy loved to help out, but this was such an important meeting.

"Okay, I'll take a look at it, but I'm not promising that I'll wear it. Retro is only in if it's distinctive retro. I won't wear it if it looks like just an old suit."

"NICE FEATHER," Producer John said, as he and Mya shook hands while standing in the reception area of Season Studios. Mya took a step back next to her mother after the introductions, put her briefcase down on the floor, and secured her artist portfolio on her shoulder to wait for the magic to begin, but nothing happened.

She smoothed the lapel on her gray tailored suit that dated back to the late thirties or early forties, Grammy wasn't sure of the exact date. It had a trim-fitting jacket with broad shoulders, large white buttons and a flared skirt. The snappy red-and-gray hat with the long skinny feather was way over the top, and Mya had absolutely refused to wear it, but Grammy had won the argument, of course.

Mya flashed him a wide grin.

Rule number one: always smile directly at the client.

"Thanks," Mya said, as she tugged on the brim of the red felt hat with the tube-shaped top. "Vintage Hollywood. It's the latest trend on the runways in Manhattan."

"Very retro. Reminds me of Katharine Hepburn or maybe Rosalind Russell in *His Girl Friday*. I like it."

A little smile. A little magic. This is way too easy.

"Thanks."

Producer John led Mya and Rita to an office down a hallway with walls lined with framed posters of other TV chefs. Bobby Fray was there, along with Emeril, Rachael Ray and several other faces that Mya recognized.

When they arrived at the office—a large room that overlooked Wilshire Boulevard and Westwood—Eric, wearing shorts and a T-shirt, and Franko, wearing almost the identical outfit, sat at one end of a long polished table. Mya hardly noticed the other two Hollywood execs seated across from them, a young man and woman. Producer John introduced the two producers as Dorothy and Lex, but Mya's entire slightly angry focus was strictly on Eric.

"Eric's been telling us some of his ideas for *La Dolce Rita*, and I have to admit, he has our attention," Producer John said.

Daggers. Red-hot daggers shot out of Mya's eyes.

Okay, not literally, but how else could a girl react

under the circumstances. The little brat had lied to her. Again! And after she had bared herself for him. Stood naked for, like, hours…er…maybe not hours, but for a really long time. And did she get to see any of his important stuff?

Hell, no.

"Did you glue those bubbles on last night?" Mya snarled as she sat down next to him at the table.

"Excuse me?" he answered, while smiling at the group.

"We made a deal," Mya grumbled. "You gave me your word."

"And you still have it."

"Oh. How's that?"

Rita broke in. "Dear, I'd like you to meet—"

Mya wasn't listening to the intros, no matter who gave them. Her full attention was on Eric.

"We'll argue about this later," Eric countered. He looked at the three producers and grinned. "Mya has a few ideas of her own. Don't you, Mya?" He made a gesture with his hands and head like she was supposed to start talking now. She refused.

"This is so like you," she told him. "Lure me into the trap, give me the candy and then go off and do whatever it is you wanted to do in the first place."

"No. You don't understand."

Producer John said, "Mya. Let's see what you've got."

She didn't move. Didn't acknowledge Eric's attempt at an excuse, if that's what he was actually trying to do. Instead, she was too busy staring at Eric and thinking about the time he had baked cookies with Franko after she had told him that she was learning how to make her own peanut-butter-and-jelly sandwich with her mom. He'd brought the cookies to school for show and tell and everyone thought he was a little genius. She'd brought her stupid sandwich, which had gotten squished in her paper bag, and everybody laughed.

Rule number two: Never trust your enemy.

Before she would allow herself to turn the same color as her hat, she was absolutely, positively sure she had the plate of cookies this time, and Eric had the smashed sandwich. No one could out-trend her. She had the power this time and knew her mother's own best future, and this nerdy cheater could *never* compete in her arena.

Whatever he had, can't possibly be as good as my pitch.

Mya stood up, removed her hat and proceeded to empty her briefcase and art portfolio onto the table.

She was determined to win the game this time, no matter what it took to get to the finish line.

ALL ERIC COULD THINK OF as Mya stood in front of the group, handing out drawings and charts and recipes, was that bathtub scene from the night before. He had played it over and over in his head until he thought he would explode. She was like a song you couldn't shake. The tune you kept humming even when you told yourself to stop. So, all right. He had it bad, but convincing her to give him a chance had to be tantamount to climbing Mount Everest during a blizzard. And now with her apparent misunderstanding about all of this, any hopes he had were certainly ground to dust.

Mya went on with her presentation. She had detailed computer-generated drawings of her mom's kitchen with a Tuscan ambiance. She played a CD in the background of the band she wanted to use for the intro and for the breaks. She went into details about the new meals and new desserts. Mya told them about the new looks she'd planned for Franko and Rita, and the celebrity guests she wanted to invite.

The whole presentation must have taken at least a half hour, too long for these Hollywood types, who kept trying to interrupt, but Mya just kept right on talking and presenting.

Mya went on and on about below-the-line costs, and how in the long-run the new set location, and all the changes, would ultimately save the network money.

The only thing the pitch lacked was any kind of spontaneity, and when Eric saw the first yawn, he knew he had to do something.

Eric stood up to get everyone's attention. Mya stopped talking.

"Let me put out a few ideas to illustrate where I think Mya's proposal can gain some added zest. Everything she's said so far is right on, but it might be lacking one ingredient. Spice."

Producer Dorothy asked, "What does that mean?"

Up until this point, she had remained silent about the whole pitch, and Eric was sure she wasn't buying either his pitch or Mya's. He hoped he could sway her into one or the other.

And speaking of Mya, she looked as though fire were going to start shooting out of her ears at any moment. Eric thought he'd better make this good and quick.

He smiled impishly at the annoyed dragon. "I'm not saying your proposal is dead on arrival, I'm just saying there's a way to spice it up. Give it a hook that's more, for lack of a better word, current."

"You're talking to me about current? You? I don't know why you're even in this meeting," Mya said angrily. "Mom—"

"He's part of this," Rita said defensively. "We should hear him out, dear."

"Why? This isn't a contest," Mya said.

Franko said, "Let's not argue. You both'a have imaginational ideas and two heads are sometimes better than the one."

"Excuse me, Franko," Mya said curtly, "but this is between Eric and me. We'll resolve it. First, the idea that we can work together is absurd. We've *never* been able to stand each other long enough to have a decent conversation, let alone work together."

As the argument grew into a family affair, Eric caught the producers exchanging positive looks. Just the kind of response he was hoping for, now all he had to do was bring it home.

"Please, please, everybody," Producer John said. "This isn't exactly what we had in mind for a meeting."

"Exactly!" Eric said in a rather loud voice. "This is exactly what *I* have in mind for the show. This isn't scripted. This is real. This is reality at its best. This is what *I* want for the show. Everybody being who they are. Arguing over color, food, setting, cooking. This is how this family works in real time and the audience doesn't need another warmed over, bland cooking show like fifteen others out there. They want something new. They want reality cooking with an Italian family who loves to argue."

"I *hate* the idea. It's stupid," Mya yelled. "It's just like you. Chaos. Madness prevailing."

"Yes, but with method to the madness. Can't you just see it?"

Mya looked angry. Her eyes were tight and her forehead furrowed. "No. I can't see it. It's ridiculous and will make a laughingstock out of our families."

"Wait a minute," Producer John said, jumping up. "Damn. This is great! Cooking chaos. Real arguments. Like a show created by Ozzy himself. I love it."

SOMEWHAT SHOCKED by the turn of events, Mya sat back in her chair to contemplate her next move. If there was a next move. She wanted to pick up her briefcase and bonk Eric over the head with it, then walk out on the whole mess. But bonking wasn't permitted now that they were all grown up.

Too bad.

Two of the producers seemed to be excited by this insane plan of his. So Mya, on behalf of the survival of her mother's show, kept her hands off her briefcase and off Eric.

Producer Dorothy stood up. "Will everyone just please relax for a minute?" A wide coltish grin spread across her face.

Here it comes. Mya had been through enough meetings to recognize that grin. It usually meant trouble, big fat trouble for everyone in the room.

"I have an idea." One by one, the group sat back down while Producer Dorothy waited for the shuffling to stop. Then she continued. "Obviously, Eric and Mya are very creative people with more than their share of artistic differences. So, in Trump fashion, I think we should let you two square off in a little family competition. I happen to like both ideas. Either one of your show ideas will come off much better than the other, or, we'll find a synthesis. We'll determine that later. But for now, I think we should do both."

The producers began to nod in her favor.

Mya's magical suit suddenly itched. Heat radiated up through her collar and down her back. She wanted to rip off the jacket and sit there in her bra. Maybe then she could get these producers to listen to reason. To understand that a family competition was strictly out of the question.

Producer John said, "We need to get this thing resolved ASAP. Let's say we all meet back here in one week. That should give you two plenty of time to put something together on tape. We'll send over a crew to get you going, plus anything else you might need."

None of this made any sense to Mya. She had pictured an entirely different outcome. One that ended with her acceptance speech at the daytime Emmy awards show.

Now, not only did she have to pull off her transformation in seven days, but she had to prove to these reality-happy producers that hers was the better show.

Well, she thought, it could be worse. At least Producer Dorothy had convinced everyone to view both ideas and, once they saw Mya's brilliant show, Eric's show wouldn't have a chance. It would be mocked, ridiculed and generally sneered at by everyone at the station. It sounded good in theory, but with Franko and Rita, the idea of turning them into the Italian Osbournes was preposterous.

Sure they argued and talked over each other, and got a bit loud, but that was part of being Italian. And maybe they were prone to moments of out-of-control madness. But what happy couple wasn't? And maybe her mom cried for just about everything. Nothing wrong with a few tears. And sometimes they would do things that were really bizarre, but didn't everyone?

All normal behavior. Nothing to get excited about. Not enough to make an entire show.

Rule number three: Never let 'em see you sweat.

Mya unbuttoned her jacket…not the whole thing. Just the first three buttons. She wasn't that desperate, yet.

As soon as the producers stood, Eric knew the meeting was over and that he'd won the first round. Not that he wanted to be in a competition in the first place, but it seemed that at this point, he had no choice. He knew just how wacky things could get between his father and Rita. Their battles were epic, and in the right setting, they'd be brilliant. Both could be sarcastic, challenging and funny.

Eric knew he'd win. He always won when it came to a competition between himself and Mya. She could never keep up the pace, and now that they were older, wiser and somewhat prone to professionalism, he had the upper hand. He could give the project one-hundred percent of his attention, while Mya always seemed to have too many ravioli on her overflowing plate. Besides, he needed to prove something to his dad. That he wasn't a flake. That he actually had some artistic talent.

Producer Dorothy said, "Until next week, then."

Mya said, "Next week." They shook hands across the table.

He could tell by the look on Mya's somewhat red face that she was as confident as he was. They were back on the beach, in the sand, shovels at port arms, ready for all-out war. And no enemy he ever faced was as sexy or as incredibly stubborn as she was.

Let the games begin.

6

"DIDN'T WE HAVE AN AGREEMENT?" Mya argued, once she and Eric were out on the sidewalk. "I mean, we came to terms with all of this and you reneged on our deal."

When he didn't answer, she stopped, grabbed him by the arm and turned him around. "Didn't you?"

Traffic was thick on Wilshire Boulevard. Mya couldn't hear herself think let alone have a decent argument with Eric with all the commotion going on around them.

He shrugged, smiled lamely and said, "Yes, but I didn't do it on purpose."

"I thought you would at least keep your word for more than twenty-four hours. But obviously, you haven't changed since you were seven."

"Oh?" he said with a sarcastic lilt to his voice. "And you have?"

Her mom and Franko were off to a book-signing for their latest cookbook and she was forced, once again, to hitch a ride in the Voodoo Van.

"Don't try to turn this around on me. You're the one who's conniving and deceitful, not me. I was always honest and true blue." She turned and walked ahead of him, head held high, chin up, chest out, well, sort of.

The suit was rather tight around her chest, so she unfastened a couple buttons and marched on.

"Oh, give it a rest. You? Honest? True blue? Maybe when you decided to take a bath in food coloring, but other than that, I don't remember anything true blue about you."

The scoundrel walked up beside her, yelling falsehoods in her ear. Among his other misconceptions, he obviously had no memory.

"It wasn't me who poured that bottle of blue in the tub, it was you."

Even though she didn't quite know where she was going, she picked up her pace and shot out in front of him.

"Yeah, well you deserved it after you stole all my Easter eggs."

Mya stopped at the corner of Wilshire and Westwood and waited for the light to change.

"I did not. I was merely taking what belonged to me, and if I remember correctly, you cheated."

"I never cheated. You were the one who watched our parents hide most of the eggs and then pretended like you simply knew where they were."

The light changed. They walked across the street in the midst of college kids toting backpacks, business types in suits and a mix of people dressed in colorful scrubs. The UCLA campus and UCLA medical center were a few blocks away. The thought drifted through Mya's head that perhaps the two of them should walk over to the medical center and find a good shrink.

"I never did that! You just can't take defeat, can you?"

"I handle it just fine. You're the one with defeat issues."

"Issues! You're the one with issues. You're the one who came up with this whole stupid reality TV cooking show idea when you thought I was going to walk away with the family glory."

She walked next to him, hat tilted to one side, feather dancing in the breeze, holding her briefcase as if it were some kind of weapon. Eric had insisted on carrying her portfolio, like that made him gallant. The man was a long way from gallant.

"You aren't going to walk away with anything. I saved your butt. You were putting those producers into a coma with all your charts and lists. At least my idea brought life back into their dead faces. Made them smile."

She wanted to cross another street, but he grabbed her arm and led her up Glendon Avenue toward the Westwood Playhouse. She didn't like him touching her, at least not now when they were in the middle of a heated argument.

She pulled her arm away. "So, who cares if they were smiling. My idea has substance, legs. It's been proven time and again to work."

"Borrring."

"What?"

"It's boring. You know my idea's better and it's going to work. C'mon. Admit it and let's just work together. Who knows what might happen if we work together." He moved in next to her and reached for her hand. She pulled it away.

"I wouldn't work with you if you were the last person on the planet."

They faced each other. "That's not true. I saw something in your eyes last night, and if your mother hadn't walked in—"

"Don't flatter yourself. There was nothing in my eyes but pure animal attraction."

"So, you're attracted to me."

She unbuttoned another button. Not only was the jacket tight, but it was far too hot. "I didn't say that."

"Yes you did. Let's go back to the house and continue where we left off." He moved in close, tight, standing in front of her just inches away, gazing into her eyes. She didn't like being that close to him, especially when she was already feeling faint from the heat. *Damn L.A. weather.* She wished she were in Manhattan. At least it was still cool enough to have a decent argument with a guy, no matter how much you wanted to jump their bones.

"You'd like that wouldn't you?"

She decided to play him a little. See if he was having the same reaction that she was. She threw him a baby-doll smile.

"Yes. It might just make up for all the nasty things you did to me when we were kids."

Not the response she was looking for.

She stepped on his sandaled foot. He was by far one of the most frustrating men she'd ever met.

"Ouch! What was that for?" He pulled his foot back so fast she nearly lost her balance.

She turned and walked away. *Jeez, he has big feet.*

"Winning. You've been in a competition with me from the moment we laid eyes on each other, and you always won. Well, this is one time when you're going to lose."

"I'll admit that there's a little competitiveness between us, but what happened in that office had nothing to do with that."

"A little? You think there's a *little competitiveness* between us? I'd say it was more like a lot. A whole lot. An amazing amount of a lot."

"What?" He stopped. She kept walking, of course, she had no idea of where she was going, but at least it was away from him.

"You know what I mean."

"Wait," he yelled, as he ran up behind her. "Wait up."

Mya stopped, but didn't turn around.

"Wait up." He came up next to her. "We've passed my van. We have to go back."

He was smiling. She hated his smile. It was way too cute and made her lose her anger momentum.

She bowed her head, trying to hide her own smile, but he caught it.

"Mya," he said softly. "We have to figure something out here, or we'll be at each other's throats for the next week. And I'd much rather be your friend than your enemy. It holds much more promise."

"Okay, friend. Are you actually going through with your insane idea?" Mya was hoping for some second thoughts on his part. "'Cause we all know how you love to be the center of attention."

She wasn't ready to back down.

"Me? I'd say that was your MO, not mine."

He started walking back down the sidewalk, retracing their steps.

"Oh? And who played doggy circus last night in the living room?" She ran to keep up with him.

"Gram wanted some entertainment. I was simply pinch-hitting."

"More like sucking up if you ask me."

"Yeah, and what do you call that outfit you're wearing?"

"Never mind my outfit." She thought she'd try to appeal to his common sense, that's if he actually had any. "Do you honestly believe your idea is going to work?"

"Yes. It'll be funnier than anything on TV. It'll save the show."

He stopped walking and waited for Mya. She caught up to him, then looked straight into those sparkling little eyes of his, and tried to appeal to his sympathetic side. "Aren't you the least bit worried that your idea will totally fail and our parents will be out of jobs? My mother would fold up and die if she lost that show. It's everything to her."

"It's the same for my dad."

"And you're willing to take a risk with their happiness?" She had him now. How could he risk his own father's future?

"I'm doing the same thing you are," he explained.

They started walking again with Mya right beside him. The sidewalk was crowded, so their hands kept touching. Every time it happened a spark shot through her, almost as if she were excited or something.

"No, you're not doing the same thing. I know my way will work. It's a proven format. Your way is a risk."

"So, who's to say I'll win?"

He had a point. She couldn't bear to have her mom portrayed as some crazed Italian woman, always arguing. Not that her mom liked to argue, or cry, or…hell, that's all her mom did, only she did it with that syrupy sweet voice that drove everyone around her crazy. Not to mention all the tears.

Of course, there was always the strong possibility

that Eric would never win the competition, so the only
people who would ever see her mom in that not-too-
sane light were the producers. And they would *never*
choose to air that on national TV. Not after all the years
her mom had portrayed herself as dignified and re-
fined. It just wouldn't fly.

They stopped when they were in front of his van. She
grabbed his arm and spun him around again. "Okay.
This time I want your solemn word and a handshake
that you won't interfere with my ideas ever again."

"I didn't interfere this time."

"Yes you did."

"Okay, maybe a little. But my show is totally different than yours. And those guys will probably like yours
better, anyway."

He grinned. *What a cutie.* She couldn't imagine how
she had ever thought he was a nerd.

"They probably will," she said, throwing him a
smirk of her own.

She had to admit she loved a good clean contest…that she won. Mya felt as light as air, and entirely
confident in her own abilities.

She stuck out her hand. He took it and it was a deal
made in heaven, or Westwood Village if someone
wanted to get technical. "Then we have an understand-
ing. We won't interfere in each other's shows."

"A deal," he said, confirming her statement, but
somehow she still didn't quite believe him.

They turned to get inside the van. Voodoo was already barking at the window. The thought of getting inside that wreck gave her a momentary pang of disgust,
but she tossed it aside, thinking this was good prepara-
tion for the game. Rivals needed to know their opposi-

tion and if that meant driving around in his filthy van, then so be it.

She told herself that this ride was strictly for research purposes.

Mya waited for Eric to open her door. He stood behind her, too close, and reached over, grabbing the handle. His arm touching her side. She could have stepped out of his way, but she chose to let herself feel his heat. A test of sorts to see if she actually had a physical reaction to him.

"Even when I lock it with a key, it doesn't really lock. If you jiggle the handle up and down a few times, you can get right in." He demonstrated his rocking trick, and on the third jiggle, the door unlatched and opened right up.

He took a couple steps back. Mya took a deep breath and let it out, trying to rid herself of the fluttering sensation coming from her stomach.

"Don't you ever worry about somebody stealing your stuff?"

"Voodoo's usually with me. And when he's not, car thieves are more interested in pricey cars. I think I'm pretty safe."

Mya climbed in while Voodoo wagged his tail and shook his head to welcome her.

Needless to say, Voodoo's spit hitting her cheek was just what she needed to reinforce her conviction that there was no way she would ever let this dog on her mother's show, *ergo,* she would have to make the show even better than better. It would have to be way over the top of phenomenal if she had a chance of winning.

As Mya settled into her favorite stinky seat, allowing herself to feel the full force of the van's delightful ambiance, she patted Voodoo on the head, thinking just what a smart chick she really was.

THE REST OF THE DAY passed in a sort of frazzled blur and, before she knew it, Mya awoke to the morning sun on the floor in her room. She lay stretched out in the middle of her printouts and charts and fabric swatches for the kitchen.

She pulled herself up from the hard floor and headed straight for the shower. As she stood there with the water running down her back, encased in glass and dark granite, she made a mental list of everything she had to do that day, including having a talk with her mom about not arguing with Franko on camera. She would have to approach her mom with logic. She'd simply tell her that if she was going to argue with Franko, to do it outside, or in a car, anywhere but in front of Eric's camera.

Then she'd tell Franko the same thing. Okay, so maybe she was interfering with Eric's show, a little. It's not like she was telling them not to argue, exactly, just not on camera.

Mya got dressed, slapped on some makeup and headed for the kitchen with all her sketches and printouts stacked neatly inside a binder. As soon as she hit the stairs she heard voices echoing from somewhere inside the house, only they weren't familiar voices.

"This is gonna be so great," Eric announced as Mya entered the overcrowded kitchen.

Mya could hardly believe her eyes. The entire kitchen, dining room and living room looked like one great big soundstage, with lights, cables and equipment everywhere.

"What's going on? I won't be ready to shoot for another week," Mya complained to no one in particular. There were several people hooking cables up to small black boxes while still others ran cable along the floor.

"This is for my reality show. The studio sent over a second unit to set everything up," Eric offered.

His camera rested on his shoulder, but thankfully, it wasn't turned on. Mya could only think of one thing. "But I need to remodel the kitchen first."

"It's all part of my show. One of these cameras will be set to interval recording so it can pick up the progress twenty-four-seven."

"You're not going to film the remodeling, are you?" Mya stepped over a black cable taped to the floor.

"Why not? It's what *really* happens, right?"

For some reason she hadn't given much thought to the possibility of being on camera. She simply took it for granted that Eric would concentrate on her mom and Franko in the studio, not at home.

Okay, she could handle this. "So, you're going to tape everything?"

"That's the plan."

But he'd said it with that touch of arrogance she knew so well. "Fine, but don't get in my way."

"Wouldn't think of it."

Mya turned and walked out of the room. She thought she'd better find a construction crew and fast, if she was ever going to get that kitchen done the way she wanted it.

She immediately found Franko outside, staring down at the pool, apparently admiring the glass tiles— at least that's the thought that ran through her head.

"Franko," she called, breaking his tile trance.

He looked up, beaming. She liked his response. It was almost as if each time he saw her he was seeing her for the first time.

"*Que bella*," he said and kissed her on the cheek. "What'a you think about this pool, hah? It reminds me of'a the blue sea in Italia. Your mamma, she's a smart woman."

"Yes. Very smart. Franko, I need some information." They sat down across from each other at the table while Mya told him some of the details for Rita's renovated kitchen.

"Ah, I got just the man for you. He gonna do a beautiful job."

He gave her the name of the contractor who was in charge of remodeling his house, Bobby Delgado. Mya made a few phone calls and within a couple hours she had a crew of four resourceful-looking men assembled for the reconstruction plan of Rita's kitchen.

At first she was a little uncomfortable when Eric began taping, but she relaxed when she looked at the whole thing as an incredibly long home movie. She even mugged for the camera once or twice.

After much discussion and some arguing, Franko and Rita came to terms with the kind of stove they wanted: gas, with six burners and a grill on the side. They also wanted three ovens, a fryolator, a smoker, a convection oven, plus two Sub-Zero refrigerators with the freezer on the bottom, which was exactly the type that Mya had in mind. They wanted a rather large, aged butcher-block island in the center of the kitchen where an extra stovetop could sit off to one side. Mya wanted the island large enough to accommodate a couple guests who could sit and watch and taste the newly prepared dishes. She wanted distressed wood for the crown moldings, brass hinges, over-and-under counter lighting, hammered-copper countertops, old world faucets, and a free-standing round table in orange-wood, with eight non-matching colored chairs.

The ambiance had to be sexy and very Italian with vibrant golds, blues, green and dark orange as the dominant color scheme. The cabinets required an upgrade to a speckled clear-glass look, and the new copper sink needed ornate colored tile as a backsplash.

"How long will this take?" Mya asked Contractor Bobby, who kept flirting with her. He was a short older man, with thick white hair and a stocky build.

"At least two months," he replied after looking over his notes. He had a rough voice, like he'd been smoking all his life.

"This kitchen has to be up and running by Wednesday morning so my mom and Franko can do prep work in the afternoon, plus have time to do a run-through of the show, to be ready to shoot it on Thursday afternoon."

His eyes widened. "What do you think this is, one of them TV shows where everybody puts a house together in a day?"

"Well. Yes. That's exactly what it is."

He threw his notes on the table. "Impossible. I'm shorthanded," he blurted. "I'll need several days just to get all the materials."

"You can have the rest of today, and most of tomorrow."

His crew sighed and shook their heads, but she could tell that Contractor Bobby was thinking it over.

"Maybe I can get you a few more people to do the work, how many would you need?" Mya asked.

"With that kind of turnaround? You're talkin' at least five or six more guys, but they'd all have to be expert craftsmen or you're never gonna pull this thing off. Plus, you'll have to make some concessions. We won't be able to do everything you want, but we can probably do most of it."

"That's all I can ask for," Mya assured him, thinking she could probably get a few carpenters from the network, but she had absolutely no idea where she was ever going to find the rest.

"Then, you've got yourself a new kitchen." Bobby and Mya shook hands, while an HMI light beamed down from the corner of the kitchen and just like that, she had stepped right into the competition full throttle, while Eric had caught the entire episode on tape.

She turned and grinned at the camera, then walked away rocking her hips as she went, feeling totally triumphant…at least until she had to find those other contractors.

ERIC WAS IN COMPLETE AWE of Mya. He'd never seen anyone so organized, so competent, so absolutely beautiful.

He knew he would have to stop focusing the camera on her and start filming his dad and Rita, but so far, she was like a magnet, and he couldn't seem to pull himself away. He had told himself to forget about her, that she wanted nothing to do with him, but he simply couldn't let go. He was the proverbial moth to the flame.

What little film he did get of Rita and his dad had been really good. He especially liked them arguing over the type of stove and the color of the tile, even though

Mya had already told them what color it would be. Eric remembered them arguing when he was a kid, but he'd assumed they were over it. They always looked so calm with each other, so loving on their show.

Actually, he was kind of happy they hadn't stopped arguing or his idea would have never worked. Who wanted to watch two loving people cook great food? That was the problem with the show…it was simply too nice. TV audiences wanted the bad and the ugly, never mind the good. America had gotten used to contentious, combative people and they now wanted to see it on their cooking shows as well. He was sure of it.

Now if he could just keep the camera off Mya.

7

By Sunday evening, Mya had everything worked out, including the ad campaign the network would run a month before the show.

She knew how she wanted her mom's hair styled, what she and Franko would wear, and she'd contacted the band and informed them of her music selection.

She'd helped her mom pick out her favorite dessert recipes, a cream-filled torta and a crisp fig strudel. Franko had decided on *filetto di maiale bardato*—a walnut-gorgonzola sauce over pancetta-wrapped pork medallions—and *riso nei carciofi gratinato in forno*—baked artichokes with a rice stuffing.

Both her mom and Franko had agreed to torque up their language by throwing in Italian words and phrases. Mya thought it was a great hook for the viewer. They could learn a delicious new recipe along with a mini Italian lesson.

"*Eh, cappo tosto!*" Franko barked, smacking the side of his head for emphasis. Not exactly the kind of Italian phrase Mya had in mind.

Rita and Franko stood in front of the kitchen stove, face-to-face, ladle-to-ladle, while Mya made mental excuses for their latest argument, as if Eric's camera could hear her thoughts.

"I am *not* 'hard headed,' you *diavolo*," Rita snapped, calling him a devil. "My sauce is never too thick. You're absolutely wrong! I've been making crab *tagliolini* for years and the sauce has always been perfect." Rita scooped the bright red cherry-tomato sauce over the thin *tagliolini*, a short type of spaghetti.

The fragrant smell of garlic wafted through the air making Mya's mouth water, but because the camera kept rolling, and her mom and Franko kept arguing, her stomach was as tight as an over-wound clock.

"You'a never cook the sauce. Other people, they cook. When you'a cook, it is never good. *Sempre male,*" Franko grumbled. "I always gotta fix. You no cook the tomatoes enough and the sauce is a mess."

Rita picked up the pot, calmly walked over to the sink and with a flurry of hand gestures she poured the remainder of the steaming mixture down the drain. "There. Now you won't have to fix my mess."

But the sauce didn't exactly fall into the sink. Instead, it splattered the walls, the floor, the counter, Rita, Franko and Voodoo, who eagerly licked up every ounce he could get to.

"You guys have to stop this," Mya warned in a terse little voice, completely outraged over their on-camera argument. They were acting like two cranky little kids. Exactly what Mya had warned them not to do. Apparently, no one cared.

Mya turned to Eric for some sense of privacy, a sense of decency, of propriety, but all she got was a perpetual smirk while his camera rested on his shoulder, recording every last embarrassing detail.

"Don't interrupt, dear. This is between Franko and me," Rita scolded.

"No, it's not, Mother." Mya nodded toward the camera trying to remind Rita of her viewers, but her mom simply threw a pot on the floor and cursed in Italian.

Mya whispered in Eric's ear. "Is this how you want America to see our parents? They're arguing over pasta sauce."

"Yeah. Isn't it great?" he said with a lilt to his voice, obviously enjoying the mad entertainment.

She so wanted to slide her hand in front of his wretched little lens and block the shot, but they had an agreement, and she was a woman of her word…most of the time, but this called for desperate measures.

Just as she was about to casually walk in front of the camera, the doorbell rang. Voodoo went into a barking frenzy and tore across the floor, slipping on pasta sauce as he went.

Grammy yelled from the other room, "I'll get it."

Rita corrected her in a loud, commanding voice. "I'll answer my own door, if you don't mind."

Rita, well splattered with tomato sauce, quickly walked out of the room. Franko followed, equally splattered. Mya and Eric were close behind.

When the group arrived in the foyer, Grammy, who never paid much attention to Rita's orders, had already opened the door. That's when Mya spotted the patrol car.

"Who died?" Grammy asked with panic in her voice.

"It's probably our neighbors, the Petricks," Rita muttered to Mya as she stood behind Grammy. "They're new to the neighborhood and the nosiest people I've ever met. We can't make a peep and they're complaining. It's like living under a microscope."

"Oh, and Eric's camera is somehow different?"

Her mother didn't answer.

Rita, Franko and Grammy all crowded in front of the door. Franko held on to Voodoo's collar to keep him from jumping on the two officers who stood in the doorway. Voodoo stopped barking with Franko's touch, but continued to lick sauce off his own chops.

As soon as the officers got a good look at Franko, Rita and Voodoo, their somewhat friendly expressions changed.

"Could you all please step out into the light where we can see you," the younger of the two officers said in a matter-of-fact voice. He was tall, with blond hair, blue eyes and a chiseled face. The serious type.

Mya was getting nervous, like maybe a lot nervous, and she didn't like the tone of the officer's voice.

"Did my neighbors call you?" Rita asked, defiance staining her voice, her hand perched on her hip. Her mom could never just cooperate. She always had to question everything.

"Please step out into the light," the other officer ordered. He was a buffed kind of guy, African-American, with a deep, commanding voice.

"Mom, I think we should do what he says," Mya offered, trying to remain calm, but actually shaking on the inside. It's not every day that two cops show up at your door and ask your mom to "step out into the light." There was something frightening about two policemen giving her family orders.

"I'm sorry if we were too loud. We're Italian," Rita told them using her best TV voice as a mound of sauce dripped down the side of her face.

The blond officer leaned in a little to get a better look at Franko, and started sniffing. "Is that tomato sauce?"

"Yeah, but it is'a too thick."

Rita instantly turned on him with fire in her eyes. "So, you have to tell even these two strangers what you think of my sauce. You never give up, do you? Always have to be right." She turned back to the officers standing on our front stoop. "Maybe these handsome young men would like to stay for dinner and they can judge for themselves," Rita said, turning on the charm.

"Can either of you play an instrument?" Grammy asked in a clear, loud voice. Mya wanted to crawl under something and hide.

The African-American officer said, "My dad taught me to play a mean accordion, but that was a lot of years ago."

Grammy took a step toward him. She came up to the middle of his broad chest. He leaned over. "I've got one up in my room. It's the very accordion that Rita Hayworth played in *Gilda*."

"No kidding?"

"Say, aren't you two the chefs on *La Dolce Rita*?" the blond officer asked.

Franko nodded, smiling.

"Yes. We are," Rita said, all chipper-like, flicking a strand of hair over her sauce stained shoulder. One thing about her mom, she never missed an opportunity to be the star.

"My mother loves your show. She watches it all the time. Is this part of the show?" He pointed to the camera, and the sauce.

"Yes," Eric instantly replied. "I hope you guys don't mind."

Mya thought for sure the officers would make Eric

stop recording and she could relax for a minute. But no. They actually encouraged him.

"No, that's fine. Love to be on your show. Some of the best meals my mom's ever cooked came from your show."

"Thank you," Franko said. "How 'bout if you come'a in. We gonna sit down to a nice dinner."

"Does one of you own that van parked in the driveway?" the African-American officer asked, obviously getting back to business.

Everyone turned to face Eric, who, of course, was still filming. "I do," he confirmed and turned off his camera. Mya graciously offered to take it from him. *It's the only decent thing to do, given the situation.*

"Seems that some of your neighbors don't like it parked out on the street. Did you know that your tags have expired and you have a broken taillight, and a missing side mirror and a crack in your windshield? Can you actually drive that thing?"

Fortunately, Mya figured out how to record, so she aimed Eric's prying camera right at him, found the zoom button to get a nice close-up of his surprised little face, and let his camera do its reality *thang.*

Officer Curtis Evans, the African-American, and Officer Sammy O'Keefe, the Irish-American, stood in the kitchen asking Eric Baldini, the Italian-American, questions while Grammy, the Eccentric-American, eagerly awaited the questioning to end. She wore a knock-off cream-and-gold-trimmed gown from *Gilda* that she had designed for retail. She looked fabulously outrageous as she leaned against the kitchen counter, stroking her golden boa. Waiting. Watching.

Smiling. Flirting with Officer Evans whenever he looked her way.

The Rita Hayworth accordion stood primed and ready in its black case for the cop to release it from its bondage and let the fun begin.

Franko and Rita had finished preparing dinner in a perfect confluence of cooperation. The amazing thing about the whole deal was that Mya kept filming, while Eric kept sweating. He seemed to be the only person in the entire family who was nervous about the presence of two incredibly patient L.A. cops.

"We're going to have to issue you a ticket for the violations and if you don't move your van, your neighbors can have it towed." Officer O'Keefe tore off Eric's ticket and handed it to him with a smile.

Eric had a look of astonishment on his face. Mya was about as happy as she could be, not because he'd gotten a ticket, she wasn't *that* vindictive, but because she had caught the entire reality moment on film. That alone was cause for celebration.

She wondered what he was feeling as she zoomed in and out for close-ups, panned the group for the total effect, then caught the little nuances of his collapse, like his tapping foot and the sweat beading on his forehead.

"Dinner, she's done. You two gonna stay, or what?" Franko asked as he held up a beautiful plate of baked salmon with pistachio sauce. There was no finer aroma in the entire world of fabulous foods than Franko's pistachio salmon, and Mya knew the two officers wouldn't be able to resist.

"That sure does smell good," Officer Evans confided, smacking his lips, his eyes focused on the plate. "We just have to radio the watch commander. We're off duty in a half hour anyway, so there shouldn't be a problem." The camera caught the gleam in his eye and the longing on his face as Franko passed the plate right under his nose.

"And afterwards you could play us a little tune," Grammy said, as she opened the black case perched on the center island, revealing the perfect treasure within. "I like after-dinner entertainment. It helps digest all that rich food those two like to try out on their family. It's a wonder I didn't die a long time ago. You'd think they'd learn a few things about modern nutrition, but not them. Too busy making a buck."

"Our food is not rich, Ma," Rita blasted. "It's traditional Italian."

"Yeah, yeah, yeah, I know what my arteries say." She turned to Officer Evans, looking demure. "Can you help a little old lady digest her food?"

He chuckled and smiled at Grammy. "Yes, ma'am. It would be my honor."

Officer O'Keefe went out to the patrol car, and by the time he returned everyone was seated around the dinner table, eager to take the first bite.

THE THOUGHT OF GETTING a ticket or maybe having his van towed was enough to throw Eric into a momentary panic attack, until he realized that Mya was filming his high anxiety. He immediately took a couple deep breaths and relaxed. She was not going to get him to overreact, at least not while he was on camera. *Somebody in this family has to appear sane.*

Eric took his camera back from Mya right before dinner, placed it on a tripod and kept it running. There was no way he wanted to miss any of the cop action at the table.

Somewhere in the middle of the third course, a pork and polenta ragu, and after both cops praised Franko and Rita's cooking for the millionth time, with emphasis on Rita's perfect tomato sauce, Mya directed the conversation to her contractor problem. Eric could only watch in amazement as her ability to get the cops interested in trying to help with her dilemma unfolded.

"So, now I'm at a complete loss where I'm supposed to come up with more contractors. You guys wouldn't happen to know anyone," she almost cooed as she batted her eyes at the two unsuspecting cops. "Would you?"

Curtis gazed at Sammy. "Actually, Sammy here used to work on movies. He was a set carpenter before he was a cop."

"Really?" Mya said crisply, turning her gaze to Sammy. Eric loved watching her in action. There was no one finer. She came from a long line of feminine persuaders, starting with Gram.

"Yeah, but that was another life." Sammy didn't seem to want to talk about it, but Mya wasn't about to give it up.

"Which movies?" she asked sweetly.

"He worked on *Chocolat*, and there was even some talk about him and one of the actresses," Curtis teased.

Bright red swept across Sammy's ultra-white skin. The entire group turned and waited for him to say something, but all he did was raise his eyebrows, smirk and go for his water glass.

"Now that's a gentleman," Grammy croaked.

Mya pushed on. "Yes, but do you still like to build things?"

He softly cleared his throat as the red blotches on his face began to fade. "Very much so. On Thursday Curtis and I leave for a week to help build houses in Kentucky. We belong to Habitat for Humanity International. The group can sometimes build a hundred homes in one week."

"Wow, that's so cool. I guess then one little kitchen is nothing for you guys. Is there any way I can get you two to help me before you leave?"

Eric could almost see the syrup dripping from Mya's voice.

Rita chimed in, "We'll cook dinner for you every night."

Look out. Eric knew these guys didn't stand a chance.

"Can I bring my mom?" Sammy asked.

"Can she swing a hammer?" Mya said, glitteringly.

"With the best of 'em."

"Well, then, bring her and anybody else you know."

"What time do we report for duty?" Curtis asked as he poured himself a glass of San Pellegrino water.

"How does ten in the morning sound?" Mya replied.

"I gonna cook a nice big breakfast," Franko added.

"Loaded with fat," Grammy moaned.

"Looks like you've got yourself two more contractors," Curtis chuckled.

Eric sat in utter awe staring at the master herself. He couldn't fully believe that Mya had somehow managed to get two cops, on their off hours, to come over and pound nails in *La Dolce Rita*'s new set.

"I THINK IT'S TIME," Grammy announced after the pear-and-chocolate tart had been consumed. "Time for our after-dinner entertainment."

The group retreated to the living room, where Eric had another tripod waiting for his ever-present camera. He set it up, and let it run as everyone took an assigned seat, courtesy of Eric's movie-magic routine.

Mya's head began to swim with ideas about Officer Evans as he picked up the accordion, wrapped the straps around his shoulders, adjusted the instrument to his body and pulled it apart to make a sound. She could visualize him like the Singing Nun from the sixties. He'd be the Accordion-Playing Cop of the new millennium. Maybe he could even be the opening act at the Blues Rock Bistro in Vegas?

Her whole body clicked with excitement as Officer Curtis Evans ran his fingers up and down the tiny keyboard. At first he stumbled and she couldn't quite make out the tune, but then he fell into the groove of it and sang out loud along with Officer Sammy, "Stayin' Alive," by the Bee Gees. Not quite the song Mya would've expected from this soul man, but perhaps his dad once had "Disco Fever."

Of course, she did wonder how anybody could possibly play this disco standard on an accordion, and what earthly reason his dad would have had to learn how to play the accordion in the first place. The whole affair was totally beyond her, but Officer Curtis did a fine rendition, a little rusty in spots, but Officer Sammy covered for him by singing harmony. And between the two of them, they would have made the Bee Gees proud.

After a while Rita started to move with the music, and before Mya could think of all the possibilities for this odd singing duo, everyone in the room, including Franko was chanting the chorus. Which was incredible enough, until her mom and Franko got up to dance.

Then Eric pulled Mya up off her chair, along with Grammy, and the three of them did some *Saturday Night Fever* moves that brought the house down with laughter. Even Voodoo seemed to be swaying with the beat. All that was needed to make the scene complete was a disco ball spinning from the middle of the ceiling and a guy dressed in a white bell-bottom suit.

Where's John Travolta when you need him?

THE NIGHT HAD BEEN AMAZING, actually, when Mya thought about it after Curtis and Sammy had left and everyone in her family had gone to bed. Matter of fact, the whole day had been amazing. And now all she wanted was sleep.

After she slipped into her pj's—a Calvin Klein little baby-blue T and matching boxers—she climbed into her soft bed, snuggled down, closed her eyes and waited for sleep to engulf her. She let out a heavy sigh as her legs slipped over the silky sheets and nestled in under her down comforter. She turned onto her right side and shifted her legs to a comfortable position, then she turned over on her left side.

A moment later she rolled over on her stomach and scrunched up the pillow under her head only to roll completely over on her back and spread out her arms and legs. Mya told herself to relax, to take deep, slow breaths, to count sheep, count pairs of shoes, count anything. She even tried her favorite method for falling asleep—relaxing each body part starting with her baby toes—but nothing, absolutely nothing, was working.

Two hours later she was up and pacing the floor. No

sleep for her. Not when all she could think of was Eric Baldini.

Her first instinct was to dismiss it as silly schoolgirl stuff, that she was merely infatuated with seeing him again, but then she realized it might be more than infatuation. The thought made her pace faster, breathe harder. This couldn't be, she told herself over and over. It was simply a momentary lust and as soon as she was back in the city, she'd forget all about him...again.

Or would she?

That was the crux of it. The annoying problem of it. She was attracted to his easygoing style, his sense of fun, his sweet face, not to mention his oh-so-fantastic body.

No, she refused to think about his body, even though it was more than fantastic. It ranked right up there with incredible.

She forced herself to think about something else. Like, how infuriating he was with his camera in everybody's face twenty-four-seven. How, like tonight, he kept the thing recording all through dinner. And speaking of dinner, he...he slurped his soup, or something equally as irritating.

Okay, so maybe soup-slurping wasn't a big enough fault to stop thinking about him. Maybe all that was needed was to simply think about his smelly van and his vicious, toothy dog.

Although, Voodoo wasn't nearly as nasty as she once thought. He was kind of cute in his own way, especially when he rocked out to the Bee Gees.

Mya fell on her bed and let out a heavy, frustrated groan. That's when there was a knock on her bedroom door.

8

"WHO IS IT?" Mya asked as she stood next to her bedroom door, not wanting to actually open it. She was in no mood for her mom, or Grammy. They'd just send her into the stratosphere with their womanly advice or, even worse, with their problems. All she wanted was to be left alone with her own thoughts, her own problems.

"I can't sleep," Eric whispered.

Her heart went into rapid-fire mode.

She opened the door only a crack, just enough so she could get a peek at him (he looked outstanding, with his tight sleeveless undershirt and gray pull-string pj bottoms), but he couldn't really see her. She was afraid she might have that totally hellcat, wanton look men recognized just before they made a move.

"It's a clear night. I thought maybe, if you were awake, you might want to check out the stars with me." He had that mischievous sparkle to his eyes. The exact sparkle he used to have when they were kids and he'd come sneaking over to her room in the middle of the night.

Hold on, girl. This could be dangerous.

She'd buried all their stargazing adventures after he'd left, and figured he'd done the same. She never expected him to actually remember any of the fun they'd shared out on that silly rooftop. It was the one thing they both had loved to do whenever he slept over. Even in the midst of a daylight battle, when nighttime came, and her mom was asleep, she and Eric would grab some bedding and sneak out to the roof. It was their antiwar zone, and it could be the one chance she now had to really check out his true intentions for both the show and for her.

"I'll meet you in five minutes," she whispered back.

She closed the door, clipped her hair up, slipped on a Victoria's Secret periwinkle silk robe—Calvins were for sleeping, not stargazing—folded up her blanket, grabbed a pillow, slipped out the door and headed for the open window at the end of the hallway.

When she climbed out the window, she expected a dark, grungy roof in need of repair. She was sure no one had been out there in years. Not that it had ever been anything but a small square of flat surface, enclosed in a three-foot-high ornate fence. Nothing more than a piece of discarded square feet that had somehow been overlooked by her mother, but found by two kids who wanted to hide from the adults in their world.

Eric stood waiting in the midst of burning candlelight, holding a bottle of champagne and two glasses. And if that wasn't enough of an incredible vision to entice a girl, a bowl filled with strawberries sat on a wooden tray, blankets and pillows littered the floor, and his old telescope waited at the end of the tiny rooftop for them.

"Where did you find that?" Mya asked, pointing to the telescope. She couldn't believe it was still around.

"Your mom had it."

"My mom? But that would mean she knew about this place."

"There isn't much your mom doesn't know about us," he said with a chuckle.

Mya blushed. "I guess so."

Mya hadn't been out on the rooftop in years. After Eric had moved to Georgia, it wasn't the same without him. Too many memories she hadn't wanted to deal with. And besides, it just wasn't a fun place without Eric. Rita had wanted to turn it into an actual patio at one point, but for some reason, she never got around to it.

But Eric and Mya had made it their own little night-time hideout where no fighting, bickering, or general meanness was ever allowed. It was a place they would come to as friends. Eric had made up the rules because he had claimed it as his hideout, and Mya desperately wanted to be a part of it.

"Champagne, my lovely lady?" Eric handed her a flute glass with a couple strawberries floating in the bubbly liquid. It looked delicious, and so did he, but she tried not to dwell on that aspect…at least for the moment. She wondered if perhaps he had something else on his mind besides stargazing. Something more romantic. A girl could only hope.

"Yes. Thank you, kind sir." Mya took the glass, walked over to the white telescope and bent over to take a look. "I see the stars are in true form tonight."

"You're not going to believe it. Move the scope a little to your right and take a really good look."

Stargazing for any normal, non-L.A. person consisted of looking up to the heavens for the Little Dipper and rings around Saturn, but when you've been raised in L.A., stargazing took on a whole different meaning.

Mya followed his instructions, easing the white tube in the correct direction, then carefully adjusting the lens to her eyesight. Suddenly, out of the darkness, to her complete amazement, sitting in a red chaise, holding a glass filled with an amber liquid, watching the water swirl in a huge pool, and tiled in the neighborhood's latest fashion, was someone who looked just like Kevin Bacon, Mya's all-time favorite actor. "Look-look-look! Oh, my God!"

She had fallen in love with Kevin back when she first saw *Footloose* with her mom when she was a little girl. He was her dream star. The man she wanted to marry when she grew up. It was all about his dancing abilities, and how he stood up to all the grown-ups. Things that were important to a kid.

She turned back to throw Eric a big fat grin. He was busy gulping down champagne, but managed a semi-smile while he drank.

Mya went back to her stargazing, completely enthralled with her dream guy, until she saw who walked up to him. "You're not going to believe this. Quick, before she leaves. If I remember right, this heavenly body was on your top-ten list."

Eric walked over to join her and peeked into the lens. "Damn, that must be Michelle Pfeiffer's double. I don't believe it." He messed with the telescope, apparently trying to get the best view. "All I can say is, wow. Look at that stellar face."

"Yes, look at it," Mya whispered as she stared at Eric.

He looked over at her. It was the perfect moment, no arguments, no competitions, just two kids gazing at the stars.

That's when he leaned in and kissed her.

All right, so he was a great kisser and as the kiss lingered on, she realized that he was possibly the best kisser she had ever kissed, with erotic tongue action, and just the right amount of...*oh, hell, now what?*

She pulled away just short of purring.

"Mya, I've been wanting to do that ever since I saw you peeking in my van," he wooed.

"You didn't even know who I was then," she mumbled, trying for some corporal composure. This wasn't supposed to be happening. This was Eric...the kid who ripped off Barbie doll heads and tormented her just by his mere presence. The guy who was somewhat of a nerd. Who needed a massive wardrobe change. Who was still in school, *for heaven's sake*.

His hands ran up the sides of her arms.

All right. This has got to stop.

"All the better," he mused.

"What?"

"All the better that I didn't know who you were. I was attracted to you, not your memory."

Not the response she needed to hear. "So you *didn't* want to kiss me after you found out who I was?"

He slipped his arms around her. She stiffened. "No. Yes. Of course I wanted to kiss you...want to kiss you. Now. Here. On our rooftop."

He leaned in for the second round, only the bell had sounded and the game was over. She stepped away from him, just as the truth came to her. "Is this some kind of ploy to get me to back out of the competition?"

"Like I would resort to seduction in order to win at a game? How low do you think I am?"

She poked her finger at his chest. "I know you, Eric Baldini. You may have grown bigger body parts, but that brain of yours still competes like a seven-year-old, especially when it comes to me. You'd use anything."

"You've got me all wrong," he said smugly.

"Oh come on. I've seen you in action, remember? Nothing's changed," she croaked and moved away from him to better look at his little conniving face. Albeit a cute face, especially in candlelight.

"Can't we just get along?"

"You sound like Clinton."

"I'll take that as a compliment."

"Take it however you'd like, but you're not going to take me," she said and gulped down the last of her champagne, grabbed up her blanket and marched for the window.

"We're not supposed to argue out here," he yelled back to her. "That was our rule."

"We're older now. The rules have changed."

And just when she was about to climb through the window, Eric announced, "That Kevin Bacon lookalike is dancing on a table."

She stopped. "What kind of a table?"

"A very small table. And he's unbuttoning his shirt," Eric said, as he gazed through the rickety telescope.

Mya hesitated at the window for a moment. Voodoo stood at her feet twisting his head to get a better look at her.

Eric said, "And there goes the shirt."

And just like that, Mya dropped her blanket along with her anger and gave stargazing on their rooftop hideout one more try.

MYA AWOKE AT SEVEN the next morning, eager to get on with her life, but the champagne and stargazing hangover put a crimp in her program. However, even with a pounding head and a queasy stomach, she forced herself to open her laptop, bring up her favorite newspapers and read all about what's happenin' now.

Then there was the e-mail from her boss marked "Urgent," but the outrageous glare from the monitor made her headache intensify, so she gently closed the thing and leaned back against the headboard. Before she could do any serious cool-hunting, she needed at least three cups of black extra-strong coffee, a couple dozen aspirin and a mega-dose of self-sucking up. The sucking-up part was merely to get her shaky ego back on track.

Okay, so she'd kissed him. Not a problem. It's not like they'd slept together or anything, not that she hadn't thought about their sleeping together. *Never going to happen. It was just a kiss.*

She had to admit that she'd lost it a little last night, what with all that stargazing, but in the end she'd managed to pull herself together, *somewhat*, and she was proud of herself for it.

They had stayed up on that rooftop for most of the night, or at least until the Kevin and Michelle stand-ins had left the party. Kevin never got any farther than his shirt, damn, and Mya and Eric never went past that kiss.

Okay, maybe they cuddled. A little. But it was cold out there on that breezy rooftop. What's a girl supposed to do?

The whole Eric experience was totally overblown. There simply was nothing there but some leftover childhood memories. Nothing to get excited about. Nothing to fret over. Nothing at all.

She just wished she had some gorgeous Wall Street hunk waiting for her back in New York. Some Donald Trump clone. Some Latin lover...*oh, wait. Eric is a Latin lover.*

The weird thing was, she couldn't figure out why she was stressing over Eric. *It's not like she was in love with the guy.*

The thought made her spring out of bed and into the shower.

She needed a run.

Mya did a speed wash, and dressed with equal zip. Normally, before she went for a run, she'd blow dry her hair and put on makeup. She hated going out looking grungy, but this morning fell under emergency status.

She pulled her wet hair up in a tight knot and clipped it in place, slipped on her new workout outfit with the cute little pink stripe down the sides of her legs, stepped into pink-and-white running shoes, and brushed on mascara and eyeliner.

Satisfied that she looked West Coast enough to face the morning, she ran downstairs, did the coffee and aspirin thing, and jogged right out the front door into the early morning sunlight.

She'd read somewhere that running was supposed to clear a person's head and give them time to sort out their problems. Mya was more of a gym chick, where she could work out at her own pace and not actually sweat, but these were desperate times. She straightened her back, pulled in a deep breath and took off down the sidewalk with total abandon.

Let the sorting begin.

The neighborhood was already alive with activity. Margie Chock, a fifty-something actor, ran past singing along to a tune no one else could hear. She smiled and nodded in Mya's direction, but never missed a beat.

Gardeners for the various estates trimmed bushes, pulled weeds and planted spring flowers. Middle-aged men and women walked their dogs, and one really older woman, Mrs. Larson, walked her cat. "Next time, I'm getting a dog. This darn thing can't keep up with me," Mrs. Larson grumbled as Mya passed her on the sidewalk. Mya simply nodded and smiled. Mrs. Larson didn't put in her hearing aid until after her walk. She hated the sound of leaf blowers in the morning.

Hancock Park was an upscale neighborhood with a mixture of red-brick mansions and old L.A. ambiance. The homes were mostly traditional, expensive and well cared for with tiny driveways and extra-large back-yards hidden behind eight-foot walls. It was a place where the streets were cleaned once a week, and your car would get broken into if you didn't lock it tight whenever it was parked on the street for more than fif-teen minutes.

A little farther down the sidewalk, Mya passed Don Eisenberg, the movie director. Don was in his sixties and walked his standard-sized white poodle every morning. Over the years, he'd owned two or three white standard poodles and always named them after his favorite singer. As Mya passed, the dog jumped up, tugging on its leash. "Brenda Lee's a little excited this morning. Her lover's just up the street. Nice to see you, Mya," Don said.

"You, too," Mya answered brightly, but kept right on going. Don liked to talk. And talk. And talk. Plus it was that whole big-dog-with-big-teeth thing again. She was actually getting used to having Voodoo around, but every now and then he'd flash his teeth and her fears would return with a vengeance.

It suddenly occurred to her, while thinking of big doggy teeth, what if female dogs were as hung-up as female humans were on looks? Was Brenda Lee's lover a little on the scruffy side, or was he one hunk of a stud?

She had to know.

She ran past a rather large iron gate and peeked inside when she heard a noise. At first she didn't see anything but ferns and flowers. But something white caught her eye so she backed up.

And there he was, sniffing the air like a true male on the prowl. Brenda Lee's white knight. The absolute, perfectly perfect stud. The poodle's poodle. The lover of all lovers. Totally white and totally full of himself, prancing around in his yard like he owned the world. Mya had to stop and admire the animal. Slim, with an elegant body, strong legs and an utterly beautiful poodle face.

He looked exactly like the doggy version of Bryan Heart, the guy with the relationship phobia.

As Mya turned the corner and headed back to her mother's house, with sweat dripping down her face and between her breasts, listening to the hum of a distant leaf blower echoing through the warm California breeze, she knew one thing for certain: running was entirely overrated!

AT LEAST THERE WAS ONE THING going well in Mya's life. The contractors had arrived. Pickup trucks, vans, table saws and burly men surrounded Rita's house.

As Mya walked in through the kitchen door, she was

thrilled to see that the demolition had begun. Two guys worked on ripping out the cabinet doors, while two other more hefty guys pulled up the old kitchen floor. Franko busied himself handing out homemade pastries and scrambled-egg burritos, while Grammy poured coffee.

It was truly a thing of beauty when all her hard work paid off. Mya wanted simply to sit back and enjoy the moment, but it wouldn't be fair to poor Eric who simply couldn't compete once she took charge of a project. He would be left out in the cold with nothing more than a silly idea.

Ah, sweet victory.

"You can *not* take my stove!" Rita's voice boomed through the kitchen as she walked in from the dining room with Bobby Delgado trailing right behind her. "Mya, do something. This silly man claims you told him to take my stove. I told him he was mistaken, but he removed it anyway. Now, tell him to return it this instant." She stomped her foot and her whole body shook.

"Mom, it's all right. You're getting the new one you wanted."

"I changed my mind. I don't want a new one."

"There's no time for that now."

"Don't tell me what there's time for. It's my show. We have plenty of time to put my stove back where it belongs."

"Mom. Calm down. Your stove is old. It's green. One of the burners doesn't even work. Bobby has a nice new one out in his truck. Don't you Bobby?"

Bobby didn't answer. His eyes just widened.

"I don't care what he has in his truck. It won't be the

same. I'm used to my stove and all its quirks. I want it back. Now!"

"The new one is part of your new set, Mom. The one we talked about. Remember?"

The countertop moved from under Mya's hand as one of the contractors ripped it out. The pounding and banging around them took on a new fury.

"I love my stove."

"Who wouldn't? Avocado-green is all the rage."

"I made your baby bottles hot on that stove."

"That's a nice memory, but now it's time to make new ones."

"I cooked my first meal on that stove. It's where Franko and I signed our first agreement."

"You signed documents on the stove?"

"It seemed right at the time. Then afterward we made love, up against the…"

Mya held up a hand. "Stop. I don't want to know this."

"Then don't take my damn stove." Rita crossed her arms over her chest and stood her ground. She could be so unreasonable.

The banging stopped for a moment and Mya spoke in a soft, calm voice, almost as if she were cooing. "Mom. You agreed on a new stove. You and Franko picked it out. You *need* a new one with a grill and all the bells and whistles like the stove on your studio set. Besides, this new one fits my Tuscany kitchen."

She grinned. One of those that's-fine-dear-but-I'm-not-giving-in-yet grins. "Okay, dear. I wouldn't want to do anything to ruin *your* Tuscany kitchen, even though changing it will probably mean nothing will ever turn out right again. But you do what you have to, dear."

Rita walked over to where the stove had once been and began to whimper, pulling out a white lace hankie to wipe up the tears.

"That went well," Contractor Bobby finally said.

9

MYA COULD TELL that the entire crew, including Officer O'Keefe and Officer Evans, was about to turn on her. She had no idea what she should do next.

Eric casually walked in from the side door with his camera perched on his shoulder. At least he hadn't been in the room when her mother had gone hysterical. *There is a God.*

Eric calmly went over to his tripod, secured his camera in place, then turned around and approached Rita, who continued to mourn her stove. He lovingly draped his arm around her shoulder, whispered something into her ear, and within moments had her laughing. Mya was completely floored.

Rita stuck her hankie in her pocket as they walked toward Mya, arm-in-arm, looking like a happy mother-and-son duo.

"Why didn't you tell me you were simply moving my stove out to clean and refurbish it? That sounds like a lovely idea, dear. It's been acting a little funny lately, anyway. Probably could use an overhaul of some sort," Rita said in a smooth, controlled voice, then smiled in the direction of the camera.

"I...I thought you knew," Mya answered, looking to Eric for some help here.

He said, "I told your mom how you would *never* get rid of something as precious as her old stove. All you want to do is give it some color, some shine. Add a few burners so it will fit in your new kitchen."

This was too much. Add a few burners? What? Did he think her mother was some kind of moron who didn't know adding burners was, like, impossible?

"What a nice idea," Rita said, caressing Mya's cheek. "You're such a good daughter. Such a simple solution, dear, I'm surprised you didn't tell me sooner."

The crew took their cue from Rita's soothing tone and began working again, while Eric escorted Rita right out the side door and into Franko's car, which was obviously waiting for her.

Mya followed, still in awe.

Rita rolled down the window. "What time do we have to meet you at Olga's?"

Olga's was the styling salon that Mya had picked out to give her mom and Franko new dos. "At one-thirty," Mya said.

"See you there," her mother chirped and raised the window on Franko's black BMW.

Mya stood there and watched as they drove away with Rita waving her animated farewell.

Contractor Bobby came up behind her. "Should I bring in the new stove now?" he asked.

"Hmm? Oh, yes. The stove."

Eric jumped in. "Yes, and could you use something off the old one? A couple knobs, or a logo? Something?"

"Good idea. That way my mom might think the new stainless Viking *gas* range, that looks absolutely nothing like the old *electric* stove is in fact one and the same, only improved somehow."

"I'll see what I can do," Bobby said ruefully.

"Thanks," Mya answered, hoping that whatever he did, Rita would be happy. She absolutely wouldn't be able to handle another Rita moment...especially on camera.

The weird thing about what had just happened was that Mya had been totally thrown off guard by Eric's ability to manage Rita, something Mya had been trying to do her whole life. And the ease with which he did it amazed her even more. Where did he learn that? Wherever he had found his smooth charm, Mya wanted to learn his tactic and fast. She didn't need any more outbursts when Contractor Bobby removed the fridge, or the dishwasher or, heaven help us, the sink. There was no telling what kind of canoodling story would come out about her mother's sink affairs.

For the next few hours, Mya and Eric and the entire crew, including Officer Evans' mother, who just happened to be an expert cabinetmaker, ripped Rita's kitchen apart. Even Grammy got into the mix. It seemed she'd always hated the "boring kitchen" and was only too happy to tear it up and throw it away.

Of course, most of the time, Mya and Eric were relegated to carrying things back and forth for the experts, while Grammy entertained everyone with old Hollywood stories. So old that Mya was sure some of the guys didn't have a clue who the star was that Gram was talking about. Even Mya didn't recognize some of the names, and she had been listening to the stories all her life. But not one of the workers stopped her, and after a couple hours they were all well versed on Greer Garson, Robert Cummings, Helen Hayes and Irene Dunne.

By that afternoon, when most of the kitchen had

been ripped apart, Mya and Eric left the rest of the details in Contractor Bobby's expert hands and the two of them went to meet Rita and Franko.

And, of course, Eric brought his annoying camera.

"I know my mom, and she's not going to let you film her while she's getting her hair done," Mya announced once they were seated inside her mom's Mercedes. At least Eric couldn't drive his van this time because it was at a garage getting fixed.

"Do I have to remind you of our truce?" Eric teased as she pulled out of the driveway and drove up the street.

"And the point being?"

"Aside from the fact that we kissed last night, we also made a bargain the other day. I thought we were helping each other now. Why else do you think I stepped in with your mom?"

"Because you had some sympathy for her distress."

"She was crying over a stove."

"She's a chef. These things happen."

"She was playing to the camera."

"No, she wasn't. There was no camera."

"There's always a camera on somewhere. You're just getting so used to them being around that you don't see them anymore."

"So, there was a camera recording the whole time?"

"Sure was."

Mya gripped the wheel with both hands and sat up straight. "Is there one recording us now? Do you have it stashed in the mirror or the cigarette lighter? How crazy are you with this reality stuff?"

"Let's not argue."

Mya cruised up Larchmont Boulevard past trendy

shops, coffeehouses, bakeries and bistros. The sidewalks were heavy with a combination of foot traffic and people sitting at small outside tables enjoying the California sunshine. She wished she could be sitting there with them, but instead she was stuck in a car with a guy who made her nuts.

"See how you are. This is a perfect example of why we can't work together. You simply don't understand the Strano women."

"Mom, it's for your own good," Mya pleaded.

"I know you have my best interest at heart, dear. But I don't want to," Rita said.

"Mom, you're not yourself right now. You've been drinking."

"Champagne is not a drink. It's a celebration."

"Fine, but there's nothing to celebrate." Mya tried to take the glass from her mother, but Rita held on tight.

"Oh, don't be such a stick-in-the-mud," Rita protested. "This is fun. I love it. Now bring that camera over here, sweetie." She let out a deep laugh as she spoke to Eric, who was busy adjusting his fifteen-pound Panasonic on his shoulder.

The aluminum foil stood straight up from the center of Rita's head like a silver Mohawk. She sat in a sleek black leather salon chair wearing a neon-blue nylon robe, with a death grip on her crystal flute glass. Smiling. Her makeup was virtually non-existent and her eyes were definitely bloodshot.

Eric hit the record button and zoomed in tight.

"Isn't this fun?" Rita announced, then guzzled the last bit of her champagne. When she finished, she held up her glass for a refill. Mya refused.

"Mom, you're going to regret this," Mya begged.

"Hush, dear. You'll spoil the shot." Rita spun her chair around so that she was facing the mirror and patted her foil Mohawk.

Eric and Mya had arrived an hour late at Olga's on Sunset Boulevard. *And whose fault was that? Eric's, of course.*

Mya poured herself a glass of champagne and downed it.

Franko, in the meantime, had consented to a stylish buzz cut that got rid of most of his gorgeous, thick black hair, thanks to Hugo, the hairstylist who was currently busy scrunching the top of Franko's almost nonexistent hair while adding gel to give him that Ryan Seacrest look.

As for her mother, hidden under the foil were cherry-red highlights, just like an aging pop singer, and once it was styled in long spikes with side-swept bangs, any woman would be envious.

But, Mya would not let the hair fiasco get her down. There were ways to work with it. Things could be done…she just didn't know what those *things* were yet.

When the hair drama was complete, it was off to the boutique where two of Hollywood's hottest fashion designers waited to redress the two hosts.

Mya was extremely cautious this time. She let Franko do the driving, while Eric followed, alone, in her mom's car.

The redressing seemed to go smoothly, except for that one time when her mother came waltzing out of the fitting room wearing a black spandex skirt and a red low-cut top. Not that her mom looked bad, she still had nice legs and, well, the woman did have cleavage, but the outfit was completely inappropriate for the show...a rock concert, maybe, but not a cooking show.

In the end, Mya convinced her to buy some colorful dresses appropriate for serious but spunky women, a few pairs of black flared slacks, a beautiful eggplant ruffled sleeveless shirt and matching skirt and a yellow cotton dress.

"And that spandex outfit," Rita told the girl adding up the bill. "Wrap that up, as well."

"Mom, you don't want that outfit," Mya said. The girl stopped adding.

"Yes I do." She turned to the girl. "Go ahead. Add it in."

"Mom. It's too young for you."

"Are you saying I'm old?"

"Of course not. It's just—"

"Not something I would wear?"

"Exactly."

Rita turned to the girl again. "Add it in, please."

"Mom. You can't wear that on the show."

"There's more to my life than my cooking show."

"Of course there is, but—"

Rita spoke to the girl who hadn't moved since the whole argument began. "I've changed my mind."

Mya sighed, relieved that her mom had come to her senses.

"I'll wear it," Rita said, grabbing the outfit and marching back to the fitting room. "And I'll take the same thing in purple as well."

Mya blamed it all on champagne residue, and sat down in a plush green chair next to Franko to wait for her pop-rock mom.

As for Franko, he came away with just the right type

of shirts, sweaters and slacks Mya had ordered, and if it weren't for his new spiky hair, he would've looked perfect.

Unfortunately, Franko liked his new do, and nothing Mya could say could talk him out of scrunching it during the fitting to give it that extra bounce.

Argh.

The next twenty-four hours passed in a construction blur with saws buzzing, people sweating and hammers pounding. The day seemed to start at dawn and end at midnight right after Bobby Delgado smashed his thumb under a box of kitchen tiles. Mya tried to soothe it with a baggie filled with ice, to keep Bobby working, but as soon as she left the room to look for a heating pad for the ache in his shoulder, Bobby sped away in his pickup.

That night as Mya slipped between her sheets completely exhausted, she thought she finally had it all nailed. Well, everything except her mother's insistence on wearing one of her spandex outfits for the taping. And Franko talking about adding some blond highlights to his hair.

Okay, so maybe things weren't quite nailed down yet, but she was sure that by tomorrow night her mom and Franko would come to their senses and go along with the program.

Minor details.

Now all she needed was one more day to finish up the kitchen and get all the prep work done and everything would be ready for the taping on Thursday morning.

After several hours of thrashing around in her bed, Mya let out a long hard yawn and fell soundly asleep until her cell phone jolted her awake.

Sunlight streamed in through the sheer curtains, causing her eyes to sting and her head to ache. The digital clock on her nightstand read seven thirty-three.

Whoever invented the cell phone is a sadist.

The whole instant communications thing was insane. Was there no place sacred in this world? Did we have to communicate with each other at every moment? Whatever happened to the sanctity of the bedroom, she mused. The privacy of one's own house?

Grace's number illuminated the cell's screen.

"I'm not answering you," Mya protested, and threw the covers over her head.

The phone rang again, and again, and again, and…

10

"GRACE. I WAS JUST THINKING about calling you," Mya said into her phone, trying for some levity.

But Grace was less than pleasant. Matter of fact, Grace was downright mean, a condition she seemed to have adopted lately. She wanted to know the details of the nonexistent Vegas campaign, and just exactly when Mya would be in Las Vegas. A perfectly reasonable request from a perfectly stressed-out boss.

Okay, so Mya had been somewhat preoccupied with Rita, Franko, Eric and, well, almost everything else, and she hadn't had time for Grace, or *trend*, or Blues Rock Bistro. But, if she wanted to keep her job, which, of course she did…she would actually have to *do* something to keep it.

She adjusted her foggy thinking by a simple head-shake, forced out a smiley face, sat bolt upright and prepared herself for some radical right-brain activity to commence. Or was it the left-brain that took on the rational elements of life? Whichever it was, she wanted the rational, sensible part to do its thing.

Mya reminded herself of how much she loved working at NowQuest. Honestly loved being plugged into the *what's happenin'* outlet of cool, and wanted to stay current with raw glamour, chic fashion and the major players.

She needed to throw Grace a bone to keep herself in the game. "Grace, um, actually, I've been working really hard on Blues Rock Bistro. Staying up late toiling over ad campaigns, talking to a wide range of people, from hipsters to punk rockers to suits, and I'm coming away with some pretty incredible stuff."

"Great! Like what?"

Mya's empty stomach swirled. *Think...think about the Bistro...Las Vegas*, but it was hopeless, her mind was jammed up with her mother's mega TV show.

That's it!

"Um, a mega-club inside the hotel, for that total big club experience. Complete with flashing lights and dancing girls and guys, dressed in scanty outfits, suspended from the ceiling. Sort of a sensory overload with three dance floors, several different theme bars and live bands, all playing at one time. Of course, the sound would be sheltered so the patrons can only hear one band at a time. Pretty great, huh?"

There was silence on the other end of the phone. Mya wasn't sure what that meant, but she was hopeful that Grace liked her idea. Hell, Mya even liked the idea. Especially the guys suspended from the ceiling part.

"Sounds fab. I'd like you to fly here today and pitch it to the client," Grace demanded. "Along with your other ideas, of course."

Mya gasped, not out loud so that Grace could hear her, but internally in her now very shaky tummy.

"Are you in Vegas?" Mya asked with extreme trepidation. She hoped it was merely a slip of the tongue when Grace said "here" instead of "there." A typo of the mouth. A brain blip. Anything.

"Yes. Got in last night, late. Brought the entire team for the meeting."

Usually, in a circumstance such as this, Mya would come up with witty repartee to buy her some thinking time. Unfortunately, this was not one of those moments. "I, um…well, I—"

"I set up a meeting for this evening," Grace announced.

Mya suddenly found herself mentally challenged. It was as if someone had closed the door on her rational brain and left her there, in the dark…brainless. "I, um…really—"

"So, what time do you think you can be here?"

"I need a little more time to prepare my findings. Like about three more days." She could hear the whine in her own voice. Had it really come to this? To whining to her boss? There was something terribly wrong with her, but she couldn't put her finger on it, exactly, but she was sure her temporary mindless condition had something to do with the fact that in the last three days she'd had virtually no sleep.

Or, she was simply losing her edge.

Either way, she had to think of some reason why she couldn't go to Vegas. Especially today. She had to stay at her mom's to make sure everything was precooked, pre-chopped and prepared. She couldn't afford any glitches when the film crew arrived.

Mya's head was spinning. Her stomach was turning. Her toes were twitching and her heart was racing. She was a frickin' whirling mess.

"Look," Grace said.

Oh, God, here it comes!

Mya really didn't like it when Grace started a sentence with "look." It meant trouble. Mya fell back on her bed.

Grace continued. "This is your baby. They like you. You speak their language. You're from L.A. just like they are. I know how much you love juggling two or three things at once, so whatever you have going on at your mom's certainly can wait a day or two. You work your best under pressure. This is pressure, Mya, at its finest and I need to know I can depend on you. Let's knock 'em dead."

Mya reacted to praise like a kitten to its mother. It made her glow. Made her purr. There was something hypnotic about it that always made her do more things than she could possibly handle. Most of the time, it worked out in her favor…but there were other times…

"You can depend on me, Grace. I'll be there."

"Good. Call me as soon as you get here."

"Right."

They hung up.

Okay, not only was it a day before the final taping of her mother's show and she had a million last-minute things to do, but now she had to leave it all, hop on a plane, and give a nonexistent presentation to a group of corporate suits.

She was determined not to let this get to her. She would simply find a way to do it all. Nothing could ever stop her once she put her mind to it.

Nothing!

VOODOO LET OUT A BIG YAWN and rested his massive head on Eric's stomach.

Ouch!

Eric awoke feeling groggy and miserable. He'd been

editing scenes on his Apple laptop using Final Cut Pro until three or four in the morning. He couldn't be sure of the exact time he finally went to bed, he'd been too tired to focus on an actual clock. He had captured some great stuff over the past few days and was anxious to get it all compressed into a half-hour show.

Fifteen minutes later, a little after eight in the morning, he and Voodoo were out on the sidewalk taking their morning walk. Actually it was more like Voodoo was doing all the walking while Eric was basically dragged from sniffing spot to sniffing spot. Not that it mattered. His mind was elsewhere. On Mya, mostly. Trying to figure out what he could do to win her over. He had thought their kiss was the beginning of a romance, but all it did was give him a momentary high.

A middle-aged man walked by with a white standard-sized poodle. Voodoo immediately turned on the charm and casually did his sniffing routine. Eric tried to hold him back, just as the poodle owner tried to hold his dog back, but the two dogs seemed to be on a mission to check each other out.

"Curb your dog," the middle-aged man scolded.

Voodoo strained on his leash, his mighty legs pushing forward, his head held high, sniffing the air. The poodle suddenly lunged for him. Eric wasn't exactly sure if the poodle was about to attack. He held on tight.

"Sorry, but he gets excited by a pretty face," Eric joked, but the guy didn't seem to get the humor. Eric grabbed hold of Voodoo's leash with two hands. He could feel the pull of the dog all the way up his arms and in his chest. Once Voodoo set his mind to something, controlling him was almost impossible.

The poodle owner kept trying to get his dog under

control. "Brenda Lee, sit. Stop, girl." But the dog seemed to have a hard time succumbing to her master's orders. Voodoo, for some reason, sat on his haunches and apparently waited for Brenda Lee to come to him. Which she did. Until her unpleasant owner pulled on her leash one more time. The poodle finally fell under submission and continued on down the sidewalk. The owner threw Eric a smug look.

Eric smiled right back at him, and Voodoo let out a couple parting yelps.

Eric knelt down on one knee next to Voodoo, pulling the dog's muscular body in tight to give him a couple pats on his chest. They both watched as the friendly poodle and her uptight owner walked away.

"There are just some women you can't have. I think she's one of them." Eric grabbed Voodoo, gave him a hug and stroked his head. "Here's the thing," Eric said, while his arm rested on his dog's muscular back. "If a chick walks away from you, that's bad. She's gone."

Voodoo blew air from between his lips.

"Now wait. There's more to this. If that same chick turns around to give you one more look, she's yours."

Voodoo stared straight ahead. Waiting. Watching. Moaning every now and then. Looking hopeful, or was that lustful? Eric couldn't tell.

They waited some more, for that one backward glance. Voodoo let out a couple little whining barks.

Brenda Lee kept right on prancing next to her owner, until she arrived at an iron gate. They stopped and she looked inside, and just when Eric was about to give up and tug on Voodoo's leash for them to go, Brenda Lee's head turned right around for one last gaze at the short black stud desperately waiting for her attention.

Eric let out a cheer, while Voodoo stood up and barked his vindication.

"You *are* the man!" Eric said, holding out his hand. Voodoo swiped his paw across it and the two of them raced back to Rita's.

"WHAT DO YOU MEAN the stove doesn't work? It's got to work. This is a cooking show. How can my mother and Franko cook without a stove?" Mya had tried to remain calm, but Contractor Bobby had a list of things that just weren't going well. And to make matters worse, whenever he would tell her a negative, he had a way of cocking his hip as if to say, *I told you so.*

She had been able to handle the smaller fridge, and the butcher-block island that was made of pine instead of oak, and she could even handle the pink paint that should have been a soft gold, but a non-functioning stove was the last straw.

"The kitchen is wired for electric. You ordered gas. There's no gas line into the kitchen, so the stove won't work," Bobby explained.

"Well, call the gas company and have them put one in," Mya countered.

"I did. They won't be here until tomorrow," he added, shifting his weight to the other hip.

"I need them here today," she confirmed, cocking her own hip.

"Not possible," he said, leaning sideways.

"Everything's possible. Bribe them," she advised, stepping up closer.

"You can't bribe the gas company," he chuckled.

"We need a gas line, now." Mya gave him her best crazed-woman stare.

He reigned in his cocky-hip attitude and said, "I'll see what I can do." Then he walked away.

The kitchen had to be put back together by the end of the day or there would be no taping tomorrow.

She took in a deep breath and let it out slowly. She told herself to relax. That she could do this. That everything would come together. That behind every cloud there's a silver lining. Where there's hope, there's a way. When one door closes...you find another door.

All she had to do was get everyone to cooperate. What could be the problem in that? It was just like any other show Rita and Franko had taped hundreds of times before. The only difference being it was filmed at home instead of inside a studio.

Simple. Easy. Nothing to it.

Then why was her bottom lip twitching?

"What's wrong?" Eric asked as he walked into the kitchen with bed-head hair. He looked as if his night hadn't been any better than hers.

"Nothing. Everything's great. Perfect, even. No worries," Mya spluttered while pressing her index finger to the corner of her bottom lip.

"Whenever you were nervous about something when you were a kid, your bottom lip twitched."

She immediately removed her finger.

"I am not nervous," she said, but her lip was going crazy.

Eric leaned in and pointed to it. "I think you are. You want to go outside where we can talk?"

Somebody had a radio blaring the latest rap release.

She nodded. He took her hand and led her outside. She wanted to hold on for the rest of time, but as soon as they were two feet from the house, he let go.

He turned to face her. "Come on. Out with it."

"I have to go to Vegas," she said wearily, while pressing her finger to her lip, again. She really hated it when her body revealed her inner frustrations. It was as if she couldn't keep anything private.

"When?"

"Today."

"Is this for real?"

"Totally."

A gray van pulled up and three guys in baggy shorts and T-shirts that said *La Dolce Rita* got out. They went around to the back of the van and pulled out a large metal cart. Two girls with blond hair and attitude jumped out of a side door. They were the food wranglers, a food stylist and prep group for the show. The girls were the two chefs and the guys, staffers. Mya smiled and pointed the way as they pushed a large cart loaded down with paper and plastic bags bulging with groceries.

Mya couldn't possibly leave now. Not when the kitchen would be filled with so many people doing so many different things. Somebody had to organize them. Had to tell them where to go. What to do. This was not the time to leave for Vegas. Her mom needed her right here.

Mya went on with her conversation. "My boss expects me to be part of a meeting sometime this evening. If I want to keep my job, I have to go, but it's crazy. I'm going to have to call her and back out."

One of the girls went back to the van and brought out a couple more filled paper bags. Franko liked everything to be fresh, and some of Rita's ingredients were hard to find. The wranglers probably had to scour L.A.

for the best produce, meat and fish to satisfy the two picky stars of the show.

Eric waited until the girl passed, giving her a nod and a smile, then he said, "But I take it you want to keep your job."

"Of course I do. I love my job. It's the best job I ever had. It's more than a job. It's my career."

"I'll come with you," Eric offered as he sidestepped another large cart filled with more groceries.

"Why would you want to do that?"

"Seems fair. Besides, there's a couple of taverns I'd like to film in Vegas."

Mya let out the breath she had been holding and noticed that her lip had suddenly stopped twitching.

"Are you sure you want to do this?"

"What time do you have to be there?"

"I don't know exactly. Sometime this evening."

"Let's just go. Now. While everybody's busy with the set. We can drive over in my dad's car, you can do whatever you have to do while I do my thing. Then we'll drive back late tonight. It'll only be four hours each way. The film crew won't be here until after twelve tomorrow. That'll give us plenty of time for a quick rehearsal," Eric said, leaning in closer so she could hear him over the high-pitched scream of a band saw.

His warm breath gave her a sexy shudder. She took a step back. He motioned for them to walk to the front sidewalk. Mya followed. A breeze caressed her face.

He turned, grinning. She thought he was simply the sexiest guy she'd ever seen, even if he was wearing last year's shorts, and a totally weird T-shirt and his hair had that 1990's look. She was learning to overlook his lack of style. His lack of cool. And anyway, there was more to a man than how he dressed, *right?*

Contractor Bobby walked past with Rita's new set of stainless pots and pans, and the rack they would hang on. *At least something was right. Perhaps it's a good omen.*

Eric gently nudged Mya out of the way, his hand lingering on her back a moment too long. She wondered if he knew the effect he was having on her.

Eric went on. "Anyway, it doesn't seem like these guys want us here today, so if you need to go to Vegas, we can be there in no time."

Mya was skeptical, but driving did seem a hell of a lot easier than dealing with the whole airport and car rental thing.

One of the contractors walked by with an open bucket of bright blue paint.

"There's no blue in my kitchen," Mya told him.

He ignored her and kept walking toward the house.

That was it. The blue paint put her over the edge. She couldn't leave. She'd have to give Grace some kind of excuse. Make up something good. Brush her off until Friday. Make her understand the urgency of the situation.

Grammy appeared at the door. "There's some Grace woman on the phone. Says she wants to talk to you. Now!"

Mya's chest tightened and her pulse quickened. "What did you tell her?"

"I'm no dummy. When a person is that intense, I know there's something up. I told her I didn't know if you were here."

She had a barrier in Gram, and she was thankful, but it wouldn't be fair to make Gram lie for her.

"That's my boss, Grace Chin. Just please tell her I'm on my way to Vegas," Mya said, smiling up at Eric.

Mya figured at least if they both went, nothing more would be filmed at home until they returned. So, this could work in her favor, after all.

A sense of relief slid through her. Now all she had to do was stop at an outlet mall on the way and pick up a new outfit for Eric. And maybe some product for his hair. I mean, she couldn't actually be seen out in flashy Las Vegas with unflashy Eric.

What would Grace think?

"Wait a minute. Did you say Vegas?" Grammy asked with a twinkle in her eye. "You two kids in Vegas? I've got just the clothes you need. A jazzy Elvis suit from *Viva Las Vegas*, and I even have a couple outfits that Ann-Margret wore. Come on with me. You two kids are going to be the envy of everybody in that town."

Mya was just about to tell her no way, when Eric grabbed her by the hand and they both followed Grammy back into the house.

Viva Las Vegas!

11

THE KITCHEN WASN'T exactly perfect, yet, but at least perfection was looming in the not-too-distant future. The stove had gas, and Rita didn't seem to notice that it wasn't her original stove. Or if she did, she wasn't admitting it. *Thank you very much.* Contractor Bobby had added a couple of green knobs from the old stove, which seemed to do the trick, at least for the time being.

Rita and Franko had made sure all the food was diced, chopped and pre-cooked. There were just a few more things that needed to be prepared, and some minor paint touch-ups, but Mya felt satisfied she could leave.

She went over a few more last-minute problems with the contractors, confirmed show details with her mom and Franko, and spoke to the directors, assistant producers, researchers, production assistants, and even some of the runners for tomorrow's show. Only after she reinspected and reconfirmed did she and Eric finally prepare for their trip to Vegas.

Mya didn't take much: her laptop, Palm Pilot, her cell phone, briefcase, a conservative brown suit, a white blouse and accessories, makeup, heels, a matching bag, underwear, a second Ann-Margret outfit and, of course, a toothbrush and paste.

Eric brought his camera.

A half hour later, Eric strolled out of his bedroom. He wore tight black pants and a bright red shirt purposely designed without the top three buttons. He carried a cropped black jacket with no lapels. His hair was combed in traditional Elvis, and black cowboy boots adorned his feet.

He looked just like the King…kind of.

Mya dressed in white tight minishorts, a fuzzy short-sleeved peach-colored sweater, white sling-back heels and a big straw hat and bag. She took his arm as they walked down the stairs and out to the BMW.

As they paraded through the kitchen everyone had some sort of reaction—whistles, laughter and catcalls, mostly.

Eric gave them a quick Elvis shimmy, then ran his hand through his hair for effect. The room exploded in applause and laughter.

To Mya's surprise, she and Eric actually looked a little like Elvis and Ann-Margret if the lighting were right and a person squinted a lot. Amazingly, it had actually been fun to dress the part, and Grammy had gotten a kick out of the whole thing.

Once they were in the car and on their way, Mya made a quick phone call to Grace to get the exact time for the meeting with the client. It was scheduled for seven-thirty. She had almost six hours to get there, plenty of time for Mya to prepare something for the presentation, and to do a little interviewing once they arrived.

There was a moment's conversation about what to do with Voodoo, but Eric instantly took care of it. There would be no doggy drool in the back seat of Franko's new car. Mya was eternally grateful. Voodoo, the dog-beast, stayed behind with Contractor Bobby to watch over the goings-on in the kitchen. Bobby seemed to hit it off with the ornery critter, so it was the perfect solution.

The traffic was running light and it didn't take any time to roll right out of L.A. and onto 15, which was a straight shot through the desert to Vegas.

ABOUT THREE HOURS into the drive, after Mya had worked on her laptop almost the entire time, Eric pulled into a rest area. He had thought the drive would be fun. That they'd spend the time catching up on each other's lives, but instead he might as well have done the drive by himself for all the conversation he'd gotten out of Mya.

"Don't you want to stretch or something?" Eric asked as he pulled the car into a space next to an old school bus that had been painted green. His attention went to the bus for a moment as he flashed on what a perfect little house it would make on his next trek across the country.

Mya looked over at him, her eyes seemed weary. "Where are we?"

"About an hour away. I thought you might want a break."

She looked around. "I've only got a few more things to add to this presentation and I'm done. You stretch. I'll stay here."

Eric opened the door. The intense desert heat immediately flew in, hitting him in the face like he had just opened a hot oven. "Come on and take a walk with me. You can finish that later."

She smiled, and he suddenly had the urge to take her in his arms, but of course, that wouldn't be happening.

"But I—"

He didn't want to hear her excuses. Instead, he slid out of the car, walked around to her side and opened the door. "You need to walk, and besides, it's hot in the car."

"You can leave the car running with the air on."

"The car will overheat."

"It's a BMW. It won't overheat."

"You won't get to see the scenic view."

"I'm not fond of the desert."

"I wasn't referring to the desert."

Mya grinned as he bent over to apparently get a better look at her.

He said, "You haven't spoken in three hours. I'm starved for conversation. Can't you just give me ten minutes of your time?"

She closed her laptop and got out. At least he'd finally come up with the right thing to say. He needed more of that.

"Okay. Where's the view?"

"I'm looking at it," he said while gazing into those smoky blue eyes of hers. He could get lost in those eyes.

"That kind of language will get you everywhere," she teased.

"Is that a promise?" He was on a roll and didn't want it to end. This was fun, standing next to her, bantering sexy innuendo. He credited this new ability to his Elvis suit. He and the King had some sort of connection.

"You and I have a hard time with promises," she advised.

"Then why do you think that I offered to come with you to Vegas?"

"I don't know, why did you?"

"Because we're working together now. We made a bargain and we're sticking to it." He leaned over, slipped his hand around her waist, pulled her in tight against his body and kissed those lips that he'd been dreaming of. He desperately wanted to touch and caress every inch of that fantastic body of hers, but of course, that wasn't possible.

Yet.

EXACTLY ONE HOUR and twenty-five minutes later, Mya rested her hand on the black rail of the moving walkway, and headed for the Forum Shops at Caesar's Palace, eager to start interviewing both locals and tourists about what they would like to see in a new hotel and casino. She had decided to try and put the feelings she had for Eric aside and ignore the kissing episode in the rest area, at least for now. She had real work to do and she couldn't let sex get in the way.

No, this time, she would be strong and not end up with a box of student videotapes when it was all over and he'd gone back to Savannah. She would not have another fling with a street-vendor type. She wanted a real relationship, but with a cool guy. There had to be one out there. She just knew it.

Eric was simply a lovable square, no matter what Grammy dressed him in, and as she watched him marvel at the faux blue sky inside the Forum, and explain how they made it and why, she knew she simply couldn't be with a man who was so obviously a nerd.

Unfortunately, this nerd could kiss.

She let out a heavy sigh.

"—and that's why they made it look like a sky. Isn't it incredible?" Eric said, as he tilted his head back to stare at the ceiling.

"Incredible," Mya mumbled, watching his mouth as he spoke, still feeling the heat of their kiss.

She forced herself to concentrate on the mission at hand.

Trend spotting, that's what this was about. The quest for trendsetters.

Mya had been to the Forum many times, both with her parents and with friends, and the place had always been a source of excitement with its variety of upscale shops, fountains and an assortment of formidable restaurants, not to mention all the picture-taking tourists.

With Eric in tow, and her strictly type A personality in full swing, she was a woman on a hunt for a fashionista, which began with the twenty-something babe right in front of her.

The happening fashion queen wore a dyed-pink raffia cowboy hat, pink flip-flops with rhinestone hearts, a Gucci oversized double-handled Bamboo Hobo bag, a pink extremely tight tee and James five-pocket stretch-denim jeans. The babe definitely had it goin' on. She was the ultimate alpha-consumer and Mya needed to talk to her.

"Excuse me," Mya said to the royal consumer in pink. "Your hat is so incredibly cool. I have to know where you bought it."

Mya had learned long ago if you approached someone with a compliment first, they would more than likely answer any and all of your questions willingly.

The girl ended up being a warehouse of knowledge.

She even had two girlfriends and a couple cute guy friends who told Mya what bands they liked, what kind of restaurants they were into, what nightclubs were hot, what their favorite TV shows were, and most of all, what casino they liked to hang in and why. Plus, Mya's instinct had worked perfectly and the pink babe and her friends were locals, making the whole encounter so worth the trip.

When she finished interviewing the group, Eric, who had been videotaping the whole thing asked, "What time's that meeting again?" They were standing beside the Fountain of the Gods. The one with huge scantily clad figures of Venus, Apollo, Plautus and Bacchus having a debate while a laser light-show went on around them.

"Seven-thirty," Mya grumbled. Even though she was now prepared for the meeting, she suddenly didn't want to go. She wanted to play with Eric...hmm, did she ever.

After all, this is Las Vegas.

Eric glanced at his watch. "I think we have a tiny problem."

"What? Is it, like, seven or something?" She glanced at her wrist. No watch. She remembered how she had forgotten to slip it on that morning. She'd been so careful about the time, but all that kissing and all that interviewing must have thrown her internal clock off course.

"No. It's eight."

The gods show went on around them. The lights dimmed. Tourists snapped pictures. Kids giggled. Lights flashed and thunder roared. Was all this some kind of prediction? A sign? The whole thing made her somewhat uneasy. "That can't be the time. Your dad's car clock said it was only five-thirty when we walked in here."

"He probably never changed it. You know, the spring forward thing."

Mya couldn't buy what Eric was saying. He had to be wrong. It couldn't be eight o'clock. It just couldn't. She would merely get the correct time from someone watching the show.

"Excuse me, sir," she said crisply to the man standing next to her wearing a fat gold wristwatch. "Can you give me the correct time?" She smiled at the charming man who would clear everything up and tell her that it was indeed seven o'clock, which would give her plenty of time to change into her special business suit. The one she always wore to the more difficult presentations. Her charmed suit. The suit that landed her the job with NowQuest in the first place...the suit—

"Five past eight, exactly," he said, holding his wrist at an angle so she could see it.

Mya could feel her insides turn to mush. Her eyes widened. Her anxiety reached up through her throat and pulled all the saliva right out of her mouth.

"I have to change," she told Eric as she headed for the nearest exit to the parking lot.

"The car is about a mile away," he said following close behind.

She stopped. He stopped. They stared at each other. She wanted to find the answer to her time problem in his face. Wanted him to tell her that it would all work out fine. No worries. But all his face said was...er...she didn't know what it said, but he sure was cute. "I can't go to a meeting dressed like this."

"Why not? *You look great, baby,*" he said, trying to sound like Elvis.

Mya rolled her eyes. It was a really bad impersonation, but she realized he was right about her wanting to change. There simply wasn't any time. Fortunately, the meeting was in one of the suites on the fifteenth floor.

"It's in a room in the Tower. Any idea where that might be?"

"No, but I've got a pretty good hunch it's not part of the Forum."

Eric grabbed her hand and the two of them took off toward the casino, dashing around clusters of tourists snapping pictures and families casually strolling by the shops.

When they got to the casino, they were directed to the elevators, which happened to be about thirty feet away. Mya's heart raced when they entered the elevator and she pressed the button for the fifteenth floor.

She pulled out her makeup bag and tried to make herself look presentable, but it was next to impossible considering that she was sweating from the run, her hair desperately needed combing, and her sweater…*oh, hell.*

She shoved the small red bag back into her briefcase. She would just have to impress everyone with her presentation and not her looks.

When the elevator door opened, the suite was, of course, all the way down at the end of what looked like a very long hallway.

MORE RUNNING. More sweating.

Eric never let go of her hand while they ran. Even

though she was late, could lose her job and looked unbelievably ridiculous, the fact that Eric was holding her
hand and leading the way made her feel confident.
Positive. Unstoppable. Assured, and any other affir-
mation she could think of while running down a hotel
hallway.

He stopped when they got to the correct door. Mya
took a deep breath, let it out and threw her shoulders
back, stuck out her chin and bullishly knocked on the
door. They were going to love what she had to say, she
just knew it.

Eric stood behind her, breathing hard.

"You're going to knock 'em dead." He rubbed her
arms. His touch actually gave her even more confi-
dence. Nothing could stop her now. She was in her
"wow" mode. She took in another deep breath and let
this one out slowly as she waited for the door to open.

Nothing happened.

"Maybe they didn't hear you. Knock again," Eric
instructed.

She knocked so hard her knuckles hurt.

Nothing. Silence.

She phoned Grace. "Grace. I'm here. Standing in
front of the suite. Did the meeting move?"

"No, it didn't move. You simply missed it."

Mya's stomach cramped. "But I have a great
presentation. I have such fabulous information to
share."

There was silence on the phone for a moment. Then
Grace said, "Tell you what. Let me see what I can do,
and I'll call you later. Just don't leave. Stay in Vegas."

"Sure, Grace. Whatever you say."

Her phone went dead.

AFTER TOO MANY MARTINIS to count, several phone calls from her always-panicked mother and a frazzled Franko, but not one from Grace, Eric and Mya found themselves at a *Blue Hawaii* wedding reception for May and Pinky Brown, two complete strangers. All the men at the wedding were dressed like Elvis and all the women were either dressed as Priscilla or Ann-Margret. There were hula dancers, an active fog machine, blue and red flashing lights and a stage filled with silk flowers and various velvet paintings of the King.

The reason why Mya and Eric were at the wedding was obvious enough, but how they managed to actually end up on stage, singing "Rock-a-Hula Baby" was somewhat of a mystery to Mya, who had absolutely no singing skills whatsoever and even less dancing skills. But there they were, gyrating to the music, flirting with each other and belting out the words that scrolled on the monitor—Eric doing a mighty fine performance.

And if that weren't crazy enough, there was a pole off to the side of the stage that Mya kept eyeing. Not that she had any intention of straddling said pole, even if it did seem to be calling her name.

What was even more disconcerting was the fact that Mya was now wearing black heels, black tights and a snappy orange sweater with a little black bow around the collar.

WHEN THE NUMBER ENDED, Eric tried to pull Mya off the stage and away from the pole. He couldn't believe she had agreed to come to the Elvis wedding so he could film it, and now she was busy making friends with a pole. And this after only three martinis. He wondered if everything was somehow his fault or was the woman always like this when she got a little drunk?

The whole episode was freaking him out. Not that he hadn't imagined some girl dancing around a pole for him, and he'd even seen a few pole dances during some crazy spring vacations, but this was Mya. His Mya. His if-it's-not-cool-I-won't-have-anything-to-do-with-it-Mya. Not some bar chick he would never see again.

Perhaps he'd had the wrong impression of pole dancing. Maybe it was the latest craze and he just hadn't caught the wave. Whatever the reason for this latest happening, it was time to call it a night.

"We're going now," Eric told her as she slid down the pole to a roomful of catcalls and whistles. He thought she looked positively amazing and incredibly sexy, but he would have liked the whole thing much better if they were alone somewhere, instead of in front of a roomful of drunken Elvises.

An Elvis tune blared from the black, supercharged speakers in the corner. Mya began gyrating again, singing some of the words, looking incredibly like Ann-Margret…or was that his own martinis talking?

"I'm just getting started," she purred in between her vocals. Her leg slipped around the pole and she fastened her hands above her head. She did it so naturally, he wondered if she had ever done this before.

But he didn't really want to know the answer to that one.

At least not yet.

"I don't think you want to get into this," Eric warned as he reached for her hand. He so wanted to get her out of there, but she was being her usual stubborn self.

She pulled away.

"But Lucky, we can have so much fun." She turned around to face him, and slid down the pole, her legs parting as she went down. The Elvises clapped and whistled.

Eric knelt down in front of her, staring into her pretty eyes. She had that dazed look, like she was completely wasted.

The Priscillas and Ann-Margrets were yelling and screaming for more. Suddenly the room had erupted into a "take-it-off" frenzy. Eric did the only thing he could think of to get her out of the room. He grabbed Mya by the waist and picked her up. She seemed to weigh practically nothing. "Come on, Rusty. It's time Lucky took you home." She fell into him, barely able to stand.

"Maybe you're right, Lucky. I'm kinda tired."

The room went crazy with cheers and applause. Eric bowed, while Mya tried to bow, but it was more of a collapse.

With one quick movement, Eric swung her around and over his shoulder.

"Ooh, Lucky, you're so strong." She giggled. "We'll be back," she yelled to the crowd, as her body relaxed on his shoulder.

More cheers and whistles.

"Maybe not," she said, caressing his back.

Eric could only think of one thing as he carefully walked out of a backstage door: he was falling in love with this incredible woman, and he would not let her go again.

WHEN MYA AWOKE, she was lying in a bed wearing nothing but her underwear. Eric was uncomfortably asleep in a chair right next to the bed, his head resting on his chest, a cream-colored blanket covering his body. She had no idea how they got there, or even where they were.

As she gazed around the room, she could tell it was in some first-class hotel—plush, extravagant furniture with a fabulous view of the strip out her window. It was still dark out, but the dazzling lights seemed to illuminate the world.

She moaned and stretched and the bed rolled like she was somewhere at sea. Apparently, last night's martinis still lingered. She tugged on Eric's blanket to try and wake him up. It wasn't right that he slept on a chair. Chivalry aside, the man looked incredibly uncomfortable. She tugged again, but this time the blanket fell off. He wore white briefs and nothing else. She stared at his muscular body for a moment in the reflection from the lights below. The whole idea of him turned her on, and she wished he would wake up so they could finally make love.

"If you move over about an inch, I think I could fit right on top of you," Eric teased.

His voice actually startled her for a moment. Like she had been caught with her hand in the candy jar.

Mya smiled, lifted an eyebrow and moved over.

12

AH, THE UNCERTAINTY of the bedroom. What would she find under those briefs of his? Was he hung well, or did he, in fact, still have that tiny little—

"Oh, my God!" Mya said out loud as she got a good look at what had been hidden under all those bubbles.

"What's wrong?" Eric asked, all cute and concerned.

"Absolutely nothing," Mya giggled softly as she prepared herself for what was sure to be the best night of lovemaking she'd ever experienced. The boy had absolutely grown into a man. "Let's get it on," she whispered as she reached down to help ease him inside her. There was nothing in the entire world she wanted more.

"Wait," he begged in a low voice. "I have a condom in my wallet."

"And I have one in my bag. It glows in the dark. Everybody's wearing them."

"Strange visual. I'll use mine, but thanks. Next time we have group sex, I'll keep yours in mind." He reached on the nightstand for his wallet.

"Only if you want to," she mumbled. The words kind of got caught up on her tongue and if she didn't know better, she'd swear she was truly wasted.

But, of course, she wasn't.

He stopped, propped himself up a little higher and looked at her. There was something so highly erotic about his position that it took everything in her not to simply reach her climax right then and there.

"I think you're still drunk. Maybe we shouldn't do this now," he uttered with a completely straight face.

"You've got to be kidding." How any man could offer to wait when the moment was hot was something she'd never experienced before, but it made absolute sense coming from Eric…always the Mr. Nice Guy. "I'm perfectly sober." Okay, so she wasn't completely sober, but she knew exactly what she was doing.

He grabbed his wallet, fumbled with the package, pulled out the condom and finally slipped it on.

"What about foreplay?" he asked. Again, way too serious with the questions.

"I believe they're a jazz band and there's no room for anyone else in this bed."

He laughed and seemed to be getting into the swing of things. She liked this attitude a whole lot better. This was the Eric she knew and loved.

Wait. Love was a strong word. She wasn't sure it was the correct word, exactly.

Maybe it was more like…

He cupped her breast, then gently rolled the nipple between his fingers, sending heat waves throughout her entire body. "I remember when these were nothing more than a promise."

Undeniably love. Big, uncontrollable love.

"You weren't supposed to notice things like that. We were babies."

He tenderly kissed each breast, taking his time, like

he wanted the moment to last. She thought she might implode at any moment.

"Little boys are perverts, didn't your mother ever teach you that? Once they discover little girls are different, that's all they dream about."

She wanted to tell him the truth about her feelings, but it just seemed so weird to say it out loud.

He kissed her long and hard. His tongue playing with hers as the intensity of his lovemaking increased to a steady perfect rhythm. Mya let out a deep groan and could no longer concentrate on a witty comeback, or her desire to reveal her emotions. Her focus was on the power of the moment.

They both came to orgasm at the same time, uttering sounds of pleasure with the release of their excitement. Mya held on tight as her orgasm ebbed and flowed, allowing herself to be completely consumed by its force. Her breath caught in her throat as her body tensed, then relaxed with complete satisfaction. The lights of the city seemed to somehow charge the excitement of their bedroom, making her want to float around the room. Dance naked on the ceiling. Shout out how much she loved him from the roof.

But as the moment wore down, he carefully rolled off of her, tucked an arm around her waist, and before she could tell him the news, her brain slid into sleep mode while focused on one final thought.

Stripper poles rock!

SOMEWHERE OFF in a foggy distance, Eric heard a phone ring. He rolled over and threw the pillow over his head. It rang again. He didn't want to answer it, no matter who it was for. How could he? It wasn't even morning yet. He opened one eye. Sunshine streamed in through the curtainless window. The sky, a bright blue. It was defiantly well into morning.

The bed moved and he flashed on the previous night and became instantly aroused. He let out a cackly moan and rolled over, remembering the feelings that had bathed his entire body with lust.

The phone rang again. He opened both eyes and sure enough, there lay Mya. Long strawberry hair covering the pillow next to him. Her beautiful, sinuous back exposed to the sunlight.

He reached out to run his hand down her spine, but she jumped with his touch, wrapping the sheet around her as she stood up, leaving him naked and cold. Not the kind of greeting he was hoping for this morning.

"Hello," she said into her cell phone.

Eric grabbed a blanket off the floor and snuggled down under it. Perhaps if he stayed in bed a little longer, she'd come over and they could play again. A man could only hope.

But the one-sided conversation wasn't going well. He detected a little anger in her voice. He had a feeling that whoever was on the other side of that call was somehow going to ruin a perfectly good morning.

"Mom, don't cry," Mya urged.

Eric slid deeper under the blanket. Crying mothers were something Eric avoided at all costs. He never could deal with his own mother's tears, let alone Rita's, whom he was sure would be completely out of control.

"Just tell me what's wrong," Mya said, as she began to pace the room, holding on to her sheet. He so wanted the thing to just slip off, but she had wrapped it so tight a mummy couldn't have looked better or more secure.

Eric tried his best to ignore the phone call, but it was useless. Whatever was going on would have a negative effect on any attempts he might make at lovemaking. And by the scowl on Mya's face, he'd say the whole day was shot. Maybe even the week.

He sat up, rubbing the sleep out of his eyes as he watched Mya grow more and more agitated, mumbling "Uh-huhs," as she walked around the furniture. From the sound of her voice he knew this couldn't be good. Not to mention the eye-daggers zinging over in his direction. He figured with everything going on, it might be a good idea if he got up, got dressed and got out of her way.

Mya gasped. "What?"

Eric grabbed his clothes and dashed off to the bathroom. Whatever was going on, he'd know about it soon enough and he'd like to be clean and somewhat dressed when he found out.

A few minutes later, while he lounged under a hot shower inside a fantastic stall of blue tile and clear glass, dreaming of the previous night and wondering how he would tell her that he loved her, the shower door swung open.

Mya appeared in front of him through the hot mist of the shower. Her hands in tight little fists, holding on to her sheet. "This is all your fault. You and your dog-beast. If it wasn't for you, none of this would have happened," she yelled and walked away, leaving the door wide open.

Eric was stunned at her outburst, especially after all they had been through. He turned off the shower, wrapped a towel around his waist and followed her out of the bathroom.

"What's wrong?" he asked in a calm, cool voice. Not wanting to ignite her any more than he apparently already had.

Mya was busy getting dressed, but not in the Ann-Margret outfit. This time she wore a pair of brown pants and a white shirt. He liked the Ann-Margret look *much* better. It suited her. He was kind of sorry he'd ever brought her bag up last night.

"We have to leave right now. This minute." She hesitated for a moment, obviously thinking. "Maybe I should take a plane and let you drive the car. Maybe I don't want to be in a car with you. Or a room. Or anywhere." She shoved the orange sweater in her bag, along with the black tights and heels. "Come to think of it, why did you agree to come to Vegas with me?"

"I—"

"Oh, my God! You planned this, didn't you?"

He wanted to talk to her. Wanted to try and understand why she was in such a snit, but ever since she was a kid, there was no reasoning once she decided on a course. "Mya, I don't—"

"Nothing's changed. You're still that same little monster you always were. And to think I slept with you last night." She walked right up to him. Eric didn't know what the hell she was going to do next—all he could think of was getting bonked in the head with his toy train. He took a step back with her approach. "Just how low will you go to win?"

"Will you please tell me what this is all about?" Finally, he was able to ask a question. But the trick was getting her to answer it.

"Don't you play dumb with me. I know you. Remember? I was there when you dumped that bottle of perfume in your father's soup so you didn't have to eat it and blamed it on me. I saw you bribe that kid to build your sand castle so your dad would think yours was better than mine. I know you, Eric Baldini. I know what a conniving, sneaky cheat you really are. But this. How did I ever fall for this one?"

"What? What did I do?"

"And to think I almost told you I loved you last night. Right there in that bed." She pointed to it with contempt. "I hate that bed. I hate all beds. If I never sleep in another bed again, I'll be a happy woman."

Eric was stunned. He never thought he could be this lucky. She actually loved him. Or at least she had last night. At the moment, he wasn't quite sure if that still held true. "Can you please stop berating me for one single minute and tell me what I did?"

She opened the door while holding her bag, briefcase, purse and an assortment of girl stuff. She turned around to give him one last parting shot, letting the door slam shut behind her. "That canine beast you call a pet destroyed my mother's kitchen. And not only that, he got Brenda Lee involved in the dirty deed and somehow her white coat is now covered in bright pink paint and Mr. Eisenberg is threatening to sue my mother for unwanted sperm infiltration. Plus, I can't get my mother to stop crying, and if there's one thing in this entire world that I can't cope with, it's my mother's tears."

Eric was at a loss for words. He didn't know what he should think about the barrage of information, much less comment on it. He watched as Mya stormed around the room, searching for whatever it was she was searching for. He thought about Voodoo and

Brenda Lee, and "unwanted sperm." One thing everyone could be sure of, if Brenda Lee was in heat, Voodoo had most definitely infiltrated.

Mya found her pink panties in a drawer, shoved them in her briefcase, swung open the door and stomped out. Eric ran for the door to try and stop her from leaving, but somehow, perhaps because the door was spring loaded, it caught his towel and slammed shut. Of course, he was out in the hallway when this happened, and the towel was caught on the other side of the now securely locked door.

He called after Mya, but she didn't, wouldn't, turn around, leaving Eric standing in the hallway without, well, without anything.

But in true Las Vegas form, before absolute panic could set in, he held on to one single thought.

What would Elvis do?

MYA HEARD ERIC CALLING HER as she walked away, but there was no way in hell she would turn around so he could try and convince her to reconsider her departure. She had to get out of there before she lost it completely. To think that she had believed him. Trusted him. Slept with him! Danced around a pole for him…wait…there had been other people in the room. She pressed the button for the elevator and tried to remember the pole dance, but for some reason all she could conjure up was a sea of Elvises. *Where'd they come from?*

She told herself to think about it later.

While she stood inside the elevator waiting to get to the ground floor, her phone rang. At first she thought it would be her mother, again, with more scary details about the disaster in her new kitchen, but her phone flashed Grace's name.

Fine.

She had forgotten all about Grace, but apparently Grace hadn't forgotten about her. She wanted to simply ignore the call and let the answering service get it, but she knew that wasn't an option. Grace would keep trying.

"Hello," she tentatively said into the phone, praying that the client had decided to go with whatever presentation Grace had pitched, and didn't need Mya's. Couldn't she have one thing go well today, just one? She wasn't a bad person, a little excitable perhaps, but she paid her taxes and was good to her mother...oh, she didn't even want to think about her mother...but didn't she deserve a break with her boss?

She listened as Grace spoke, watching the lights behind the numbers flash as the elevator descended into hell, no doubt. "Okay. It took a little doing, but we have a meeting set up at ten." *Definitely hell.* "Same place. That gives you a good hour to get there. Please be on time. They won't wait for you again."

Mya sucked in her courage. "We'll need to reschedule for another day. Say, like Monday. Monday morning is good for me. Anytime. I simply can't make it today. Really sorry that I put you through all of this, but when they see my fantastic presentation, it'll have been worth the wait."

"Are you serious about this?"

All professionalism flew out the now open elevator doors, and slot machine bells and laughter flew in. Groveling came to mind.

She had indeed arrived in hell, so Mya did the only

thing she could think of to get herself out of the fire. "Grace? Are you there? Grace? Did you say something? I can't—"

Mya hit the power button on her phone and shoved it into her briefcase. She walked through Caesar's casino and out the front doors with her self-confidence in a tailspin, but as she slipped into the back seat of a cab, she was sure she would regain it on the flight back to her mom's.

So, ALL RIGHT, Eric had to admit that running down a hallway in a busy hotel with nothing on hadn't exactly been the best way to start his day, but he'd managed to find a newspaper outside a door. And never mind that as he was snitching it, a gorgeous brunette opened the door before he had a chance to cover his *package*, and she had to call her two roommates over to take a look at the naked guy outside her door delivering their newspaper. And so what if they wouldn't give him *their* newspaper, but instead gave him the only towel they could spare—a washcloth—and he had to wait outside their room while a convention of romance writers walked by, ogling, before housekeeping could get to him with a robe and a key to his room.

It wasn't as if the whole experience were Mya's fault or anything as ridiculous as that. She probably didn't hear him yell for her as she stomped up the hallway. The quiet hallway. Where she couldn't have been more than ten feet away when he first called out her name.

Okay, so he was a little miffed at the woman, maybe a whole lot miffed at the woman, but he'd get over it. And the Voodoo mess couldn't be all that bad. Rita always overreacted. A trait Mya seemed to have inherited. But, he loved her and she loved him, at least she had said she had in the middle of the night.

But as he drove up 15 on his way back to L.A., doing ninety-five, he couldn't help but wonder if he could actually survive this kind of love.

MYA WAS ABLE TO GET A FLIGHT without too much trouble, but as the miles whizzed by beneath her feet, so did her self-confidence. It was a feeling she simply wasn't familiar with and didn't know quite how to handle.

She tried reading a magazine to find her inner strength, but all the articles seemed to be focused on fashion and trend. She even tried to have a conversation with the guy sitting next to her, but he was preoccupied with eating a piece of his shoe.

Mya stared out the window at the mountains below, waiting for some inner peace. Some modicum of self-confidence to return to her battered ego, but nothing came. She wondered how she'd ever let herself get talked into the side trip to Vegas in the first place. It was so unlike her to delegate and trust other people to take on her job. To miss meetings. To make excuses. To hop in bed with the enemy.

Well, whatever that was, she wasn't ready to give up. Not yet. *I mean, how bad could the kitchen be?*

She reached for *Marie Claire* and flipped to the article on Britney Spears and what she wanted next. All Mya had to do was read the article and everything would be good again. Because, after all, if Britney could have a Vegas indiscretion and come out of it all right, so could Mya. It was simply a matter of proper planning and the right clothes.

When Mya arrived at the airport all happy and chipper, a real limo waited for her right in front of baggage claim. She eagerly jumped into the back seat, and in no time she stood in the middle of what had to be the absolute worst mess she had ever seen.

Everything she'd painstakingly learned from Britney flew out the open kitchen window.

"Mya, please don't cry," Rita begged, wrapping her arms around her daughter as they stood in the center of the kitchen calamity. "I hate it when you cry."

13

RITA, MYA AND GRAMMY STOOD in the middle of the kitchen in a tight little circle on the only clean spot on the floor.

A fine turn of events, Mya thought as her mother tried to tell her that the catastrophe of the kitchen wasn't so bad.

"I'm sure we can find a way to clean it up before the rest of the crew gets here," Rita suggested.

Mya looked around. She had been standing in the same spot ever since she'd walked through the kitchen door and that was almost an hour ago. She simply couldn't move because every time she tried to, she'd start to cry again. Full-out sobs would come rushing out whenever she stepped on a piece of food or discovered another paint mess. So she merely stood there, glued to the clean spot.

"Oh, come on, Rita," Grammy said. "For once take those blinders off and get real."

Gram was right. Mya couldn't fully believe that one surly dog could do such an incredible amount of damage. There were several colors of paint spilled on her beautiful cream-tiled floor, splashed on the walls and cupboards. Bright pink paw prints tracked across the once-shiny copper countertops and into the sink. Food was everywhere, even up on the tops of the glass sconces. Eggshells, various vegetables, raw pasta, cooked pasta mixed with tomatoes, pieces of artichokes, torn paper bags, sugar, flour, a half-eaten pork roast and some kind of unrecognizable food matter littered the counters, floor, table and chairs. It looked as if some sort of food bomb had gone off.

"And just when do you expect the rest of the crew?" Mya asked in between sobs.

Rita glanced at her chunky pink wristwatch, while her bright red highlights danced through her hair. She wore a clingy top that showed off her ample breasts and gold-striped pants flared down to her red toenails. She absolutely did *not* look like her sweet self. Just another catastrophe to add to the mix on the floor.

"In about twenty minutes."

Mya nodded, unable to speak.

"The Side Room, that band you hired…a nice group of boys, by the way…they came by early this morning to set up, but of course they left when they saw the kitchen. I really tried to get them to stay. I even told them you'd be angry if they left, but that didn't seem to make a difference. I'm sorry, dear."

Mya had somehow totally forgotten about the band. "That was fine, Mom."

"Good. At least something worked out."

Mya raised an eyebrow.

It was a good thing that Voodoo was nowhere in sight or she'd have to strangle the mangy beast.

Or worse.

However, she did want to know where the creature was hiding. "Where *is* Voodoo?"

"Franko took him to the groomer. He was a mess."

"I bet he was," Mya said, wiping her tears away.

"What's our next plan of action, sweetheart?" Rita asked, flipping a strand of red over her shoulder.

"A bulldozer," Grammy mumbled.

Rita ignored her and waited for an answer from Mya, as if Mya actually had an answer.

Was this her test? That mother-daughter moment when Mya was supposed to swoop in and save the day? Come up with a new plan? Be the hero? The bombshell? Like Sydney Bristow, or better still, the bride in *Kill Bill*?

Mya pulled out her phone and called Contractor Bobby. He'd certainly know what to do. She was proud of herself for being able to think under extreme circumstances.

"Hello," he said in that deep husky voice of his.

"Bobby. Hi. This is Mya." She almost whispered it in some breathy Marilyn Monroe voice she never knew she had.

"Mya Strano? What's wrong? Are you sick? Your voice sounds funny."

Apparently, breathy wasn't working. She cleared her throat. "No. No. I'm fine. It's just that we have a little problem here."

Grammy rolled her eyes.

"What's wrong? I checked everything myself before I left last night, and it was all good," he grumbled.

"I'm sure you did, and I'm sure it was, but it seems that Eric's dog, Voodoo…you remember Voodoo, don't you?"

"Yeah. Sure. Great dog. The guys loved him."

"Well, anyway, he might have gotten a little carried away after you and your team left and, um, well, he kind of got into the paint and—"

"I told those guys to cover those cans. Did something get spilled?"

"Actually, a lot got spilled. Do you think you could come over, like now, maybe?"

"Sorry, but I'm in Malibu today working on a job I can't leave. If you can wait till day after tomorrow, I can swing by—"

"That won't work. How about sending over somebody from your crew?"

"Everybody's up here. Sorry, but I just can't help you today."

Mya's only hope hung up.

Usually under these kinds of stressful situations, she would use her contingency plan. A quick solution to an unforeseen problem. The dependable backup plan was sometimes even better than the original plan. She prided herself on always being prepared for the unexpected. The unpredicted. The surprise lurking in the wings waiting to throw you off course.

Unfortunately, this was not one of those contingency plan times.

This was so seriously unexpected that she never even gave a plan B a second thought. Besides, there was no time in her tight schedule for anything to go wrong.

"Is he sending someone over, dear?" Rita asked, trying to force a smile.

Mya took a deep breath and let it out.

"Not today, Mom."

"So? What? Are *our* fingers broken? Instead of crying in our pasta, let's get some brooms and clean this place up," Grammy offered.

"I think there's more to it than that, Gram," Mya countered. "What about the ruined paint, and all the food's been half eaten. We don't have time to prepare that again."

"So, we have to figure something else out," Grammy continued, looking right at Rita. "You're getting lazy, anyway. So is Franko. Neither one of you make anything from scratch anymore. You both cheat. No wonder your ratings are in the toilet. You don't cook!"

"I'm too busy to do that much cooking," Rita argued.

"Busy with all that sex, that's what. That's all you and Franko do anymore. Sex. Sex. Sex. You should start your own sex show. Then your ratings would go up."

Rita blanched. "Ma. We do not have sex all the time." She paused. "Occasionally. When the moment is right. But that's none of your business."

Mya interrupted. "I don't want to know this."

"Why not? You got something against sex?" Grammy asked.

"No, I—"

"Then take my advice. Be like a bunny rabbit while you're young so you won't be ridiculous, like your mother, when you're old."

"I am not old!" Rita shouted.

"Mom. Gram. We don't have time for arguing."

"Why not? All we have is time. She can't cook, or should I say, *won't cook.*" She looked directly at Rita.

"Ma. You make my blood boil. You know that?"

"Good. Cleans out your veins from all those rich foods you eat. I keep telling you to start cooking lighter, but do you listen to me? No. Same old stuff." She bent over and picked up a piece of what once was a yellow cake. "Look at this. Probably a pound of butter in here. You're killing your viewers. That's why you have low ratings. They're all dead!"

Rita's face turned a bright red. Mya knew she was ready to blow, so she moved in between the two women.

"Wow! It's a mess," Eric's voice echoed from behind her.

"You can say that again," Grammy snapped, then abruptly turned around and sat down on the only clean chair in the kitchen. Rita flipped her hair back over her shoulders and watched her mother take a seat, mumbling something in Italian under her breath. Mya couldn't quite make it out, which was probably a good thing.

Now that they were somewhat calmed down, Mya could concentrate…on Eric.

The man of the hour had returned.

She slowly turned to face him. Anger mixed with adrenaline burned through her body. She could feel her heart pound in her throat. She took a step toward him. Her eyes narrowed.

He took a step back.

Smart man.

"Now, wait a minute, Mya. Before you go jumping to conclusions," Eric stammered as he continued to back up, slipping on whatever it was that he stepped on.

She just kept walking toward him, seeing red. It was times like these that she wished she had taken karate lessons, or kick-boxing, or at the very least, mastered the art of hair-pulling.

He continued to back up. "I've given this a lot of thought and—"

"I don't want to hear your thoughts," she hissed. "You and your dog have ruined my mother's one chance to save the show."

He tilted his head. He could look really cute when he tilted his head.

This wasn't one of those times.

"That's not exactly true. We still might be able to save it."

She took another careful step toward him, not knowing exactly what she would do when she caught up to him, but she was sure instinct would kick in. "Since when did 'we' become a concept? There *is* no 'we' in this contest. There's your stupid reality tape that makes our two families into raving lunatics, and me with my tried-and-true method that will showcase their superb cooking skills."

He smirked, albeit a tiny smirk, but a smirk nonetheless.

"From the looks of the kitchen, your 'tried-and-true method' is pretty much in the toilet."

The smirk was his giveaway. She now had her proof that this whole thing had all been planned. He'd probably even had some kind of arrangement with Grace. There never was a meeting in Vegas. She wasn't even in Vegas. The whole thing was a complete hoax, *and I fell for it!* She was sure of it. That smirk, that tiny Eric smirk had said it all.

She squinted and just kept walking, careful not to slip on the mound of sliced cooked pears peeking out from an overturned pie dish. "Oh, and who put it in the toilet?"

"You can't blame this on me. I had nothing to do with it. I wasn't even here. Too busy in Vegas ripping you off of the pole you danced around. Or can't you remember?"

"That's my girl," Grammy shouted.

"My Mya, dancing around a pole?" Rita gasped, then to Mya she said, "I always wanted to do that."

It was too much. Mya lunged for him, reaching out trying to catch him, but the little worm ran out the side door.

But as she tried to catch the smirking schemer, a better idea flashed before her eyes. It came to her as soon as she ran outside and spotted his stinking van. She knew exactly what she needed to do. What the plan B should be.

His cassette tapes.

Those vile tapes of her mother with her hair plastered to her head, or the argument with Franko, or the night everyone danced to accordion music in the living room. She had to get them. If she couldn't be in the competition with him, with something upstanding and decent, then he certainly couldn't be in it without her with his Osbourne odyssey.

As he backed up against his father's car, apparently getting ready for the worst, Mya spun on her heels and ran back into the house.

"What the—" Eric mumbled behind her as she made her way through the rubble that once was a magnificent kitchen and up the stairs to his bedroom.

It only took a minute for the *chaser* to become the *chased*. She could hear Eric's hot and heavy footsteps right behind her. "You can't do this," he yelled. "We're not kids anymore."

"Oh, yeah. Watch me," she yelled back as she tore down the hallway and burst into his room. The white Apple laptop was perched on the oak desk just waiting for her to snatch it up. His cassettes and a DVD sat right next to it calling her name. She snatched everything up just as Eric entered the room. Fortunately for her, the window was open. She ran for it before he could get to her and dangled the laptop out of the window.

Eric stopped so abruptly he almost fell over. "You wouldn't."

"I would."

"But everything I've ever shot is in that computer. I don't even know if I have backups for some of that stuff."

"Oops. You should have thought of that before you trained Voodoo to destroy my set."

"You don't honestly believe I had anything to do with that mess."

"He's your dog, ergo, it's your fault. You trained the beast."

"To destroy a kitchen?"

"Seems logical to me, considering your background."

"So, you actually believe I trained him to eat your set? Is that it? And how do you think I accomplished this amazing task?"

He took a step toward her. She leaned out the window farther. "Oh, I don't know. How did you train him to spin a basketball on his nose?"

The laptop slipped. It was heavier than she thought it would be, especially when it was suspended out of a window. She pulled it up tighter in her hand.

"That's different. It's just fun. Voodoo's been spinning stuff since he was a pup. Come on. You really don't want to do this."

"Yes I do," she said with conviction.

Okay, so maybe she didn't really and truly want to drop his laptop, but she couldn't let him know that, at least not now when they were in the middle of mortal combat.

"Aw, come on. You're making me nervous."

"Then it's working."

"Can't you at least bring it inside?"

"Not until we come to one final agreement."

The laptop slipped again. This time Eric must have seen it because the look on his face said it all. He really did *not* want to lose that laptop. Mya wondered why she hadn't thought of this little number sooner. Like when she first walked into the kitchen. She could have just hid the damn thing instead of dangling it above the earth. Her arm hurt.

But, in truth, this was much more fun.

He took a step back. "Okay. What are the terms this time?"

Good question, only she hadn't actually thought that far ahead yet. To actual terms. She never dreamed he would cave so easily. Okay, she needed to come up with something fast because her arm was getting unbelievably tired, even burning a little, and getting those sharp little tingly feelings that ran up and down, making her fingers weak. Did he have extra batteries in the thing or what?

"First, um, you have to let me keep your laptop and your cassettes, and the DVD so I know you won't bring them to the meeting tomorrow."

"If I do that, our parents won't have anything. Their show will be canceled. Is that what you want?"

"*No.* I don't want their show canceled, but I don't want it turned into some kind of cooking comedy either. I hate reality shows. Especially when the people in them look like fools."

"But you haven't even seen what I've done yet. Our parents don't look like fools. I wouldn't do that. What I've got is really good."

"In whose opinion?"

"Mine."

"You don't count."

"Then let the producers decide. Don't we owe it to our parents?"

"We owe our parents the best we can give them. What you've shot is most definitely not our best."

"Why don't you sit down and let me play it for you? I know you'll change your mind. Can't you give me at least that much?"

"And if I hate it?"

"Then we'll come up with something we can both agree on. Maybe some kind of combination of both show ideas. Just don't drop that laptop."

At least he was being somewhat reasonable. Besides, her arm was really burning now.

"You lie."

"No. I swear on…what we had last night. I'm telling you the truth." He took a couple slow steps toward her. Whenever she thought about their lovemaking her insides turned to mush. She so wanted it to be something real, something true, but she just couldn't be sure.

"How do I know you were telling the truth last night?"

He didn't have to say anything, he just looked at her and she could see the honesty in his face.

She relaxed. "Okay, but if I hate it—"

"I'll erase it and destroy the cassettes."

He took another step toward her and she wanted to fall into his arms and forget about everything but his touch. She didn't look at him and see a nerd anymore, she only saw his true character shining through, and from where she stood, she liked what she saw.

Mya turned toward the window to pull in the laptop and just as she did, Voodoo, with a bright red bow tied around his neck, came bounding into the room and headed right for her.

"Voodoo. Noooo," Eric yelled, but it was too late.

Everything moved in slow motion as Voodoo leaped up on her.

She freaked.

Slobber hit her cheek and mouth causing an instinctive reaction to wipe the disgusting stuff off.

She lifted her hand as the laptop slipped from her grasp. She swung around, desperate to grab it, and when she did, the cassettes and the DVD went tumbling out of the window as well. For a brief moment, she felt as if she were going out the window with everything else until Eric grabbed her and pulled her back.

They watched as Eric's laptop crashed on the hood of Franko's BMW with a thunderous thump, bounced off and fell on the cement with a sharp cracking sound that Mya could feel in her bones.

The pretty white laptop splintered and chipped, and pieces of it littered the driveway. The cassettes exploded when they hit the ground, propelling unwinding tapes to cover a pile of discarded kitchen plaster and debris. The DVD rolled over to the edge of the driveway, spun for a moment and died right on the thorniest cactus plant in her mother's garden.

Suddenly there was complete silence. No cars passing. No leaf blowers. No helicopters. No sirens.

Just dead silence, at least until Voodoo huffed and whined.

14

THE REST OF THE PRODUCTION CREW arrived shortly after the laptop incident, took one collective look at the kitchen, wished everyone luck and left, leaving no one from the network behind.

Eric picked up the remains of his laptop, packed Voodoo in his van and drove away without saying a word to Mya, who was simply too shocked to speak.

Rita took Franko's car into a body shop for the dings and scratches to the hood. Franko picked her up and the two of them went out for lunch.

Grammy disappeared into her office, and Mya jumped out the window…er…not literally, but she wanted to.

However, being of sound mind…a somewhat debatable issue…instead of self-destruction, she locked herself inside her bedroom and spent the afternoon reviewing her life so far.

It was in times like these that an ambitious, creative and incredibly competitive woman had to lie back and get perspective. When a girl searched for that silver lining. That open door. That ray of sunshine. Or the reason why she could have been so stupid as to hold Eric's laptop out of a window.

Could she be more brainless? More idiotic? More childish?

What moron holds a laptop out of a window?

"This moron, that's who," she said out loud.

She rolled over on her bed, staring up at the blank white ceiling, trying to remember the first time she'd done something this stupid, with every intention of pulling back at the last minute.

Case in point: the Transformer incident. She had *never* intended for the damn thing to actually go into the toilet, but it had, and once it was there, she wasn't going to stick her hand in that dirty old toilet to get it out, so she had flushed.

"Totally stupid," she said out loud. Actually, she'd never liked that Barbie anyway, and the haircut Eric had given her doll was kind of cute. But it was the principle of the thing that had made her mad. Made her want to get even.

And, of course, there were more stupid moments. Almost too many to list, so she decided to focus on the *really* brainless ones and leave the rest for another day's perspective.

She started with her first memory of standing up on a chair and threatening her mother with emptying an entire box of salt into a pot of chili if she didn't get…she couldn't remember what it was that she had wanted. But she did remember how it had ended. The open box had slipped out of her hand, fell right into the chili, and she had gone to bed without any dinner. Her mom had cried all night, and of course so had she.

It wasn't that she was trying to justify Voodoo's crazy behavior, or the fact that Eric wouldn't buck up and take the blame for his insane dog. Or that she still thought the whole Vegas trip was a surreptitious way for Eric to get her out of the way—although, his setting up Grace was kind of preposterous.

None of that seemed to matter now. It was more her dislike of her reaction. That she'd stooped so low. That she had felt it necessary to get even. It was the same feeling she'd had toward him when they were kids.

She didn't react this way toward other people. With other situations. It's not like she went around throwing her boss's laptop out of a window when Grace would trash her ideas in front of a roomful of co-workers. Although…could her initial reaction to Grace's urgency in Vegas have been a way of getting even? And what about accidentally missing the meeting? She remembered something about how *there were no real accidents.*

She shuddered at the thought.

No.

She was better than this.

She knew how to behave. Knew how to control her anger.

At least she thought she did, but whatever happened to turning the other cheek? Looking the other way? Counting to ten? Biting your tongue? Being the better man, or in this case, the better person?

It took awhile to go over some of the other major screw-ups of her life—exactly two hours and fourteen minutes…apparently there had been a few more than she'd first thought…and sometime right around the memory of her eighteenth birthday party when she was caught kissing Patrick McCafferty, her then-best friend's boyfriend, and caught by said best friend, Ronnie Lombardo, who had lured him away from Mya in the first place, her cell phone rang.

She sat up and grabbed it, thinking it might be Eric forgiving her for being…well…herself.

She answered without checking the caller ID window, slapped on a happy face, as if he could see her, and said in a cheery voice, "Hello?"

"Hello, Mya," Grace grumbled into her ear. The absolute last person on the entire planet Mya wanted to talk to.

"Hi, Grace. How's Vegas?" Somehow she still wanted to hold on to the idea that the whole meeting thing was a setup.

"Not too good."

Grace had an edge to her voice.

"What's wrong?"

"Everything. We lost Blues Rock Bistro. They've decided to go with some other company I've never heard of. I tried to convince them they won't be happy with anyone else. That we have the best solutions, but after waiting for meetings from my star employee, I can't blame them."

Mya's heart sank even lower, if that was possible.

Grace continued, "Listen, I really hate to do this over the phone, but I've given it a lot of thought and you've given me little choice in the matter."

Mya didn't like the sound of this. She had to defend herself. "Grace, I was just—"

"I'm sorry, but I'm at McCarran Airport and I can't hear you very well. Can you hear me?"

"Loud and clear," Mya said mildly.

"I want to get this said before I get on the plane. Mya, I'm afraid I'm going to have to let you go."

The words hit her right between the eyes. She

wanted to make light of it, like she didn't care and say, "Go where?" But she stopped herself.

Grace continued. "I'm really sorry about this, but maybe you'll take this time to think about your priorities. Lately, they certainly haven't been about your career, or your future."

"I understand." *Who am I kidding?* "I'll be in next week to clean out my desk."

"Not necessary. I had it cleaned out today and shipped to your apartment. I've got to go. My flight's boarding. Listen, I enjoyed working with you. Too bad it had to end this way. Keep in touch. And if you need a reference, just ask."

She hung up.

Mya lay back on her bed and stared at the clean white ceiling and sighed.

"STUPID JERK," Eric yelled as he leaned on his horn. He was stuck in a busy intersection and the guy in front of him had just cut him off, nearly causing Eric to run into the back of his SUV.

Of course, if Eric had been paying more attention to the road, he probably would have seen the guy in the first place, but he was still raging over his laptop and now apparently taking it out on L.A. traffic.

Not a good combination.

He decided that he needed to calm down or he'd be the cause of some major accident, for sure.

He turned on the radio and Elvis filled his van with "Love Me Tender." He turned it off just before Elvis could sing "Love me true…"

There would be no Elvis tunes in his van. Not now. Not ever.

He pulled into a strip mall and parked.

Relax. Deep breath. Shake it off.

The whole Mya thing had gotten to him more than he wanted to admit. And her latest get-even installment had left him both angry and confused.

At least he'd managed to grab the cassettes from the camera that he had set up on interval taping in Rita's kitchen. He still couldn't believe that Voodoo could have done that much damage. He didn't know who or what did, but he knew his dog well enough to know that Voodoo only went for food, which he'd eat, and not mindless destruction.

Eric was on his way to his dad's house thinking about the last week, the last day and the last moments trying to understand it all. He couldn't quite believe what had just happened—all his work, gone in a heartbeat. Just like that.

And she didn't even apologize. Not one word. Nothing.

Okay, so it was Voodoo's actual fault, but still, *who holds a laptop out of a window?*

He could argue that she wouldn't purposely have dropped his computer. No sane person would do such a thing. Maybe that was the answer. The girl wasn't sane.

At first he'd thought she was bluffing, but now he'd never know the truth. Voodoo had stepped in and forced the play.

He decided the woman had apparently never grown up. Not emotionally, anyway. She was a little girl caught inside a fabulous woman's body.

Was that it? Had this whole thing simply been a bad case of lust? Was he just another guy reacting with his hormones instead of his brain?

He needed to know the truth. Needed to know if he and Mya had something real going, something honest like love.

But the girl couldn't hold her temper, or her need to get even. Not that he'd been much better in those two categories, but she seemed to bring the worst out in him.

And sometimes, the very best.

Voodoo rested his large head on Eric's shoulder.

"Yeah, I know. You didn't mean it." Eric stroked the dog's head. Voodoo yawned, letting out a sigh.

Suddenly, Eric wasn't so sure about anything. About what he felt for Mya, about his need to prove something to his dad, or his stupid idea of reality cooking. Perhaps Mya had been right all along and he should have merely sat back and let her do her thing.

Helped, even.

Okay, so he'd established that he was a complete idiot when it came to figuring out TV shows and women, especially when both of those things were tied up with Mya Strano.

All he knew for sure was he needed to get away from her. Away from Rita's house and the mess in the kitchen. Had to be on his own to think about what he really wanted…and so far, nothing rational had come to mind.

When he finally focused on his surroundings, he realized that he had stopped in front of the small computer repair shop he'd been looking for. If it hadn't been for the guy in the SUV, he'd still be driving around L.A. looking for the place.

Moments later Eric stood in front of a lavender counter under a sign that said Help Desk.

"You've got to be kidding," the guy behind the counter said as he gazed at the cracked and broken laptop.

"I need to know by the end of the day if you think you can get anything off of it," Eric begged.

The tall, yellow-haired guy with three tiny silver hoops through his left eyebrow grabbed the iBook and swung it around. A white chip flew off the counter. The guy picked it up and handed it to Eric. "This might be all you get, dude."

Eric took the piece and shoved it in his pocket. "Just see what you can do."

"I'll call ya," the guy said. "Name's Gary."

Gary took Eric's information, picked up the battered electronic marvel and disappeared through an open doorway. Eric stuck his hands in his pockets and walked out, hoping Gary was some kind of computer genius.

When he arrived at his dad's, he had the house to himself. The contractors were apparently gone for the day and his dad was nowhere in sight. He immediately played his interval cassette in his dad's TV, hoping that he and Voodoo would be vindicated.

It wasn't ten minutes into the tape when his dad walked in. "So, the car don't look too bad. They gonna fix it up for tomorrow. What about the show? You got anymore ideas up'a your sleeve?"

"Fresh out."

"What you watching?"

"I set the camera up in the kitchen before I left for Vegas and it shot thirty seconds of film every ten minutes. I want to see what really happened last night."

Franko sat down on a leather chair, Voodoo spread

out at his feet, and Eric sat cross-legged on the floor in front of the TV. The two men watched as Rita, dressed in a baby-blue silk robe and slippers, opened the side kitchen door, let Voodoo out, and proceeded to pour herself a glass of milk while she opened her mouth for a mighty yawn. In the very next scene, Rita was nowhere to be found, but the side door was still wide open. Then nothing but an empty kitchen. Eric hit the fast-forward button thinking this was all a waste, until he saw a flash of white. He hit Rewind, Stop, Play.

Brenda Lee pranced into the kitchen, immediately jumped up on a chair and then onto the kitchen table, which was covered with tiny soup cartons, bags of flour and various ingredients for the show. Voodoo walked in behind her, sat on his haunches and watched as Brenda Lee proceeded to rip up everything she could sink her teeth into.

"Gotcha!" Eric yelled.

The real Voodoo came up behind Eric, stared at the TV and growled.

Brenda Lee's piercing bark echoed through the room as she jumped off the table and headed for the large white painter's bucket in the corner of the room. The TV Voodoo turned to watch her, growled and barked a couple times, but Brenda Lee paid no attention to him.

The real Voodoo continued his growling in Eric's ear.

Eric hit the pause button and Brenda Lee's mouth froze as she grabbed hold of the bucket.

"It's okay, buddy. Calm down," Eric told his dog. Voodoo stood, eyes trained on Brenda Lee's image. Eric patted his dog's muscular chest.

Eric's cell phone rang.

It was Gary from the computer repair store.

"Hello," Eric said, but it was more of a question than a greeting. He really didn't want any bad news. Not now. Not when he was feeling somewhat vindicated.

"Well, what do you want first?"

"Just lay it on me, man," Eric said, but he hoped against all hope that the news was good.

MYA DECIDED TO CLEAN UP the kitchen. Somebody had to. Her mom had threatened to help, but then disappeared when it came time to actually do the work. Mya didn't mind, though—it seemed like she deserved to clean up Voodoo's mess.

She had a large garbage bag going and an industrial-sized dustpan. Her hair was pulled off her face and tied back in a scrunchy, and after working for about an hour, she was covered in just about everything that was on the floor or stuck to the walls, including the pink paint. Somehow this was not how she had intended to spend her vacation.

Just as she was about to dump a particularly heavy load of junk into her overflowing garbage bag, her mother finally appeared all glammed up. She looked jaunty in a fabulous pink, red and white pop-art-graphic, long-sleeved, low-cut dress, a strand of long pearls around her neck, matching earrings and pink stiletto heels on her feet. Obviously not cleaning attire.

"They're here, dear. You might want to wash your face and change your clothes," Rita suggested, giving Mya the once over.

"Who's here?"

"The *L.A. Times.*"

Mya dumped her dustpan into the bag. "Come again?"

"The reporter is here, and he brought a really cute photographer. They're out front parking. How do I look?" She twirled around like she was excited over the whole publicity opportunity and wanted Mya to join in on the fun.

"What possible reason would you have for allowing them into your house? Especially now?" Mya scooped up mushy figs and some unrecognizable oozing yellow substance into her dustpan, then dumped it all into the bag. Only she missed and it dripped down her leg, causing Mya to wince at the cool, gooey feeling as it settled between her toes.

"They heard the news and want a story."

"About what? This kitchen? Eric's laptop?"

"Why would I tell them about any of that?"

"Okay, then what? Your new show? Because there is no new show thanks to me. I'm sorry I couldn't come through for you, Mom. Really I am." She swept up broken dishes and chewed-up foil.

"Don't worry about it, dear. That's not why they're here. Although, I was going to add that part to the interview, but no matter. You're a clever girl. You'll think of something before that meeting tomorrow. I'm sure of it."

"I'm glad somebody is," Mya mumbled.

"What did you say?"

"Nothing. Now, tell me why there's a reporter parking in front of our house?"

"It's the latest buzz all over town. I thought for sure you'd have heard about it and be just a tiny bit angry at me for not telling you first. I wanted to, but you were always so busy planning and working that the right moment just never came up. And then yesterday, when you ran off to Vegas. Well. Anyway. It's actually done wonders for our ratings. I don't know why I didn't think of this sooner."

Mya wiped a strand of hair off her sweaty forehead and gazed at her mom, who seemed to be completely oblivious to the mess around them. Instead, she was almost euphoric. A complete reversal of how she was only a few hours before. Whatever happened to that crying woman Mya had heard on the phone just that morning?

"Perhaps we should sit down," Rita offered, looking around.

"Mom. There is no place to sit. Just tell me what's going on." Mya leaned against the counter after pushing shredded paper and mashed bananas out of her way. She was actually feeling a little nauseous and could use a break.

Rita took a deep breath. "I decided to marry Franko."

"Excuse me?"

"What I mean is, Franko and I are finally getting married. We were going to do it all along, but I wanted to finish the tile in the pool first."

Mya stared at her mother. She never could understand the woman's logic. "And the reason being?"

"I would think it would be obvious to you, dear."

Mya gave her a sidelong glance, still confused.

"For the reception, sweetheart. I couldn't very well have a wedding reception and not have Italian tile in my pool. In this neighborhood? I'd never hear the end of it."

Mya knew her mother's neighborhood perception was somewhat out of whack, but that wasn't what sent Maya reeling. She tried to remain calm in the face of absurdity.

"So you and Franko are getting married, and you're having the reception here, and when exactly is all this supposed to happen?"

"I've always wanted to be a June bride."

"And Franko is going along with this?"

"Why shouldn't he? We're in love. Always have been. It just took us a while to fix up our two houses. Then when I changed my hair color, well—" she blushed "—things just heated, I mean, speeded up. When you get to be our age, you have to think rationally."

"And you think this behavior is rational?"

"Of course it is. Never mix real estate and love. Just ask anyone."

This was all coming too fast for Mya. She needed to sit down like her mother had suggested, but everything was covered in garbage.

Rita looked off for a moment. "Perhaps we should have had this talk before you left for New York?" She returned her gaze to Mya. "No matter. It's never too late for a mother-daughter moment. Anyway...where was I?"

"Love and real estate."

"Right. Love is never reasonable. If it were, you wouldn't be standing in front of me sweeping up Voodoo's mess. It's your way of forgiving Eric. But I don't have a clue as to how he's ever going to forgive you. Throwing his laptop out of the window was a bit extreme, even for you, dear."

"Mom, that's ridiculous."

"What is, dear?"

Mya replied, "That love is never reasonable."

"Actually, it isn't...reasonable. Why do you think little boys dip little girls' pigtails in inkwells?"

"Mom, there are no more inkwells."

"You get my point. It's their way of telling the girl they're in love with her. You and Eric just never got past the inkwell stage. That's what all this is about. You love each other, and the spitballs are flying."

"Don't be silly. Lovers don't act this way. They're sweet to each other. Kind. It's all about candlelight, flowers and love songs."

"Whatever you say, dear, but something made you throw his laptop out of a second-story window."

"Actually, it was Voodoo's fault."

"Darling, you can't blame everything on that poor animal. He'll get a complex."

Mya didn't know how to respond to that, so she went back to the original topic. "Where are you and Franko going to live?"

"Right here, of course. You don't seriously think I spent all that money on those silly tiles for someone else to enjoy, do you?"

Mya slapped her forehead. "Silly me!"

The doorbell rang. "Okay, honey. Enough of this. We've had our bonding moment. Do you understand everything now?"

"Yes. Everything's crystal clear."

"Good. I'm glad we had our little talk. Now, get yourself cleaned up. And put on something stylish. I want my daughter to look like her fabulous self for the camera. You've proven that you love Eric, now forget about this kitchen and let's go and talk to the reporter. I have an entire crew coming in later to clean this mess up and Bobby will be over tomorrow to do the heavy reconstruction work."

"I thought he couldn't come back until next week? That he had some big job over in Malibu?"

"He did, dear. But *I* took care of it."

Mya caught the intonation in her mother's voice. It sounded like Don Corleone, Attila the Hun and Carol Brady all in one.

She wanted to ask her mom the details.

But then again, maybe she didn't really want to know....

15

"YOU TWO ARE GETTING MARRIED?" Eric asked after he turned off his camera and stuck it on a tripod. He never saw it coming. His dad hadn't even mentioned it, but that was the kind of relationship he seemed to have with his dad. The long-distance type.

It was about nine o'clock at night and Franko, Rita and Grammy were hard at work cooking together in Rita's brand new kitchen. Eric's camera captured their every movement on film. The marriage announcement was one of those movements.

"Yes. In June," Rita added, beaming.

Eric so wished that Mya was there to hear and see this, but Rita said she'd left for a drive about an hour before, never really telling anyone where she was going. Rita had even tried to phone her, but Mya must have turned her phone off.

This whole ad hoc filming began when Grammy called Franko and told him to come over and to bring Eric. Apparently, Contractor Bobby had sent over a clean-up crew, and aside from some dried errant paint and chipped plaster, the kitchen looked pretty great. Grammy thought they should at least think about filming something for the meeting the next day.

That's when it happened. Spontaneously, once they

were all in the kitchen. Like some jam session for cooks. Grammy started in with Frank Sinatra's wedding to Mia Farrow, what they wore and eventually what they served at the reception.

Right in the middle of her story, Rita took off with an idea for a new show.

It took exactly one hour for Franko and Rita to gather all the ingredients for the wedding feast and ten more minutes for Eric to set up his camera and the proper lighting and sound.

Of course, Gram changed into a white-lace wedding dress. "Another knock-off I designed," she said while she showed off the large bell sleeves and the short hemline for the camera. She also wore white stockings and white shoes. The woman was an incredible warehouse of old Hollywood trivia, and Rita had finally decided to use it to her advantage. "Dean Martin said once that he had Scotch older than Mia Farrow, but Frank didn't mind the jokes. He was in love with the little thing. She was as cute as a button with those big round eyes and that supershort hair. I knew her mother, Maureen O'Sullivan, a real Hollywood bombshell. How she loved her little Mia. Anyway, the wedding was a traditional Italian feast with lots of pasta dishes and Italian cold cuts. They had the shindig at a producer's house, Edie Goetz. But Frank's mom, Dolly, made the final decision on most of the food."

Franko, who had prepared a tomato sauce on the new stove, looked into the camera and said, "We gonna make it all. Ravioli. Scaloppine. Green lasagna. Fettuccine. Sausage gnocchi, and garlic and olive oil scungilli. The best!" He kissed the tips of his scrunched fingers.

"We're going to make these fabulous dishes with

less fat," Rita explained as she spoke to the camera, grinning over at Gram. Rita actually sparkled when the camera was turned on. The ultimate star. "And I'm going to show you how to turn these wedding dishes into superhealthy foods just by adding a few simple ingredients."

"So stick with us, kids, 'cause we've got the wedding feast for the Chairman of the Board. Right here," Grammy said, then she giggled.

For two hours, the three cooks prepared the feast while Grammy told Rat Pack stories. They each chopped, fried, boiled and sautéed and in the end, plated each entrée so that it looked like a wedding, using silver-rimmed white dishes, a white tablecloth and silver accessories.

That's when Franko and Rita announced their own wedding, which came as somewhat of a shock to Eric. Actually, it was more like a shock wave that hit Eric. He wanted to sit down, but his father came over wiping his hands on his white apron.

"Rita will be my stepmother. Mya will be my stepsister. There's something wrong with this family album," Eric mused as he thought about making love to his...stepsister. "Is that legal?"

"Sure, it's legal."

Eric looked at his dad and wondered if the man had read his mind. *A scary thought.*

Franko went on. "We got the license and everything."

"Great. That's great, Dad." But he didn't say it with much enthusiasm and Franko must have caught it.

"So what? You got a problem?" Franko scolded.

"A problem? Me? No problem. But I do have a question." Rita had walked over to the back of the kitchen. Out of earshot. "You two seem to argue just a little bit more than most couples. How's that going to work?" Eric asked, totally serious. He couldn't imagine how they would ever stay married.

"A match made in heaven," Gram said, grinning. Rita had walked back. She whispered something to Gram and the two women started laughing.

"If you don't argue, you got no life. It keeps the heart pumping, and the veins clean. A person's gotta stand up for what they want, drive the idea to the end, or they gonna get run over by what they don't want." Franko put his arm around Eric's shoulder and led him out the side door, away from the women. Obviously, he didn't want them to know what he was about to say.

A rush of excitement swept over Eric. He was finally going to get some advice from his loving but somewhat distant dad.

He leaned in to hear the words of wisdom from a man he'd admired all his life and had tried to emulate and please. A man whom he loved with all his heart. His dad. The man among men.

"Whatever you want to tell me, Dad, I'm listening."

Franko stopped and gave him a strange look. "Good, but I don't got nothing to say."

"Then why did we walk away from the women?"

"Because sometimes those two make me *pazzo*. Insane, you know?" He twirled his finger next to his head. "All the time they talk and laugh. Like two little girls. I don't know what my life is gonna be like once I move into Rita's house. I'm a little bit scared. What you think? Huh? Is it a good idea to sell my house, or what?"

It was the first time in Eric's entire life that his dad had asked him for his opinion.

"Yes, Dad. I think it's time for a change. You've lived alone long enough. I think you'll be happy living with Rita and Gram. They're great."

Franko looked at him, sincerity written all over his face. He said, "You know something? I think you are right. It is time for me to be around love again. It's a good game, this love game. It's the most important thing you will ever do with your life."

"What's that?"

"To give your heart to a woman."

"Isn't it kind of scary? What if she doesn't love you back?"

"Believe me, it's worth the risk."

They hugged, and Eric knew their relationship would never be the same again.

Eric and Franko walked back in the kitchen. Franko turned to the two women. His eyes were a little moist as he said, "I think everything, she's finished up. Let's eat! *Mangiare, tuti famiglia.*"

Eric hit the record button on his camera, focused in tight and joined the group at the new table to enjoy the feast. He couldn't help wishing that Mya were there, but obviously the woman wanted no part of him.

AFTER AN AMAZINGLY RESTLESS night where all Mya could think of or dream about was Eric, and occasionally Kevin Bacon...and even Elvis popped up once singing "Rock-a-Hula Baby"—a song she'd never even heard of up until two nights ago—Mya awoke to Grammy standing over her, holding up a white suit.

"It's time to wake up," Grammy said. "Or we're going to be late for the meeting."

Mya rubbed her eyes and stared at her plucky grandmother, who wore white mother-of-pearl glasses, large pearl earrings and a jazzy white pantsuit with wide lapels and satin buttons. Her makeup flawless.

"What's this all about?" Mya asked, as she stretched out the long night's kinks.

"White shows purity of power," Grammy explained. "And, we're gonna knock 'em dead, just like those women did in *First Wives Club*."

"But we're not wives, and they aren't our husbands," Mya countered.

"Don't mess with my motives. We're wearing white. It gives us that angelic quality."

"But white is *so* last year," Mya grumbled.

Her grandmother leaned over and looked her right in the eye. "Mya, I learned something a long time ago. It's what kept me going in Hollywood when they told me I'd never make it."

"They actually told you that?"

"No, but it sounds good for interviews. Don't interrupt."

"Yes, ma'am."

"I start trends. I don't follow them. Look at all my creations and the rage that happened afterward. There's only one thing you have to remember in this world. Lead, never follow and everything will go your way."

"That's the secret to happiness?"

"No. Happiness is another lecture. When we're not in such a hurry, remind me and I'll tell you the secret. But right now I'm teaching you how to be confident about who you are."

"But I am confident," Mya said, but she knew Grammy could see right through her.

"Not from where I sit."

"All right. I'm not confident at all. I lost my job."

"What?"

"I got fired."

"So, who wants you to work in New York, anyway? You got a job right here."

Mya sat up in bed. "Yeah? Like what?"

"You have to manage your mom's show."

"What show? There is no show, and if there was any hope for a show, I threw it out of a window. I'm a complete jerk."

Grammy sat down next to Mya on the bed.

"That's not what I see."

"What do you see, Grammy?"

"Okay, since you asked. I see a beautiful girl who has a lot of talent but she's wasting it on everybody else."

Grammy stood up. Mya reached for her hand to hold her back.

"Wait, isn't there anything else? Something you want to tell me about my character? My career decisions? My love life? Some sage bit of wisdom you want me to learn?"

Grammy thought for a moment, then shook her head. "No. I think I covered enough. The rest you'll have to figure out for yourself. It's all part of becoming a woman. Nobody can do that for you. Not even me."

Mya let go of her hand. Grammy walked over and hung the white suit on a hook next to the door, then started to walk out of the bedroom.

"But Gram, I don't have anything to show these producers."

Grammy turned around. "Maybe not, but at least you'll look good," she said, then turned around and left the room.

Mya had to smile at her grandmother's unyielding spunk.

She slid out of bed and headed for the shower, wondering if she would ever be able to figure this whole womanhood thing out, because lately, she seemed to be in an adolescent tailspin.

Two hours later, the two power-angels arrived at the production office. Rita, who'd looked incredibly beautiful, upbeat and positive, had left earlier with Franko. Now Grammy—why she had insisted on coming along was a complete mystery to Mya—was as feisty as ever as she walked along the hallway. While Mya was totally apprehensive about both the meeting and seeing Eric.

Mya had thought he would have phoned her, or shown up at the house, but he never had. And every time she'd picked up the phone to call him, she'd chickened out. Hell, she even drove over to his dad's house the night before and sat out in the car for about two hours imagining herself walking up the front steps, but in the end she couldn't think of what to say, so she circled the block a few dozen times and went back home.

And now it was time for the meeting and all she wanted to do was run. Jump on a plane and fly back to New York City. Not that she had anything or anyone waiting for her in New York City—she was in between street vendors and jobs at the moment—but she just didn't want to face Eric.

Okay, wait, she could do this. She'd had to face many opponents in her day, many guys where *she'd done him wrong*. Well, maybe not *many*, but enough.

Okay, one. One guy, but he'd so deserved it after she caught him kissing her new best friend.

Er, what goes around actually does come around.

So, she'd finally learned her lesson. *Now what?*

She thought it was a bit odd that impressing the producers was really the last thing on her mind. No matter what happened, she now knew her mother would land on her feet and save her own show. She really didn't need Mya to do it for her. Never had. Her mother was her own person with her own goals and no matter what, she was a survivor.

Mya wished she could be that sure of herself, that honest about the really important things, but she was still a little fuzzy on where to begin the search.

While she and Gram walked down the hallway to the meeting room, escorted by the receptionist, Mya wondered if Eric would even show up. *I mean, why should he?* Perhaps he'd gone back to Savannah, or Vegas where he could be the next hot Elvis impersonator. After all, he sang a mean "Viva Las Vegas."

Perhaps she wouldn't see him again until there was another family crisis. Of course, the thought of actually facing him after what they'd done to each other completely terrorized her. Made her stomach knot up, her pulse quicken and her body sweat…or was that from the memory of their lovemaking? She so wanted that to continue. Wanted more of his touch. His kiss. His—

Her breath caught in her throat at the very idea of his naked body on hers. She took a misstep and stumbled.

Grammy grabbed her arm. "Never let 'em see you sweat."

The receptionist walked in front of Mya and Grammy.

"I'm not worried about the meeting," Mya said mildly, tugging on her creamy white jacket.

"I know." She winked and grinned. Grammy's whole face lit up. She was positively radiant.

"Am I that obvious?"

"Of course you are. The women in this family wear their hearts on their sleeve."

"I'll try to keep mine rolled up for the meeting."

"Don't bother. It'll only ruin a perfectly good suit."

The two women locked arms and continued their walk to the meeting. It was at that precise moment of obvious emotional chaos, and when she knew there was little hope for any kind of relationship with Eric, that she heard somewhat peculiar music echoing through the long hallway. She could barely hear it at first, but as it grew louder with each step there was the distinctive sound of accordion music.

Her pace quickened as "Stayin' Alive" filled her head with recent and somewhat embarrassing memories. But she didn't care. She just wanted to see Eric. Needed to see him.

She wanted to run down the hallway, but Grammy held tight as they continued their walk to the meeting room.

As she stood in front of the door, holding on to Grammy, listening to the familiar notes, feeling her pulse quicken with each chorus of the Bee Gees' hit, she knew one thing for certain.

Eric was in the building.

16

To her absolute disappointment, Eric was not in the meeting room. Matter of fact, she was sure she'd seen him slip out the opposite door the moment she walked in.

And the music had stopped.

She wondered if she'd actually heard it at all considering she'd destroyed Eric's laptop herself. Perhaps it had just been wishful hearing.

The memory of that laptop hitting the ground gave her an instant queasy feeling.

She took a deep breath to try and make it go away, but it didn't help.

She swung her white bag onto her other shoulder, then swung it back again.

"Relax, dear. It's all worked out," Rita whispered in her ear. *The woman has some sort of sixth sense.*

"Why isn't Eric here?" Mya asked Franko.

"He's got a lot to do. He gonna go back to school today, so he no can stay."

Mya's eyes instantly watered and there was a pesky lump in her throat. Something she never thought would happen.

So, all right, they had a minor disagreement, but it was all part of the contest. Part of the game. But to leave without a *see ya, adios, ciao,* or a *go to hell,* well, it was unbelievably unacceptable.

How could he?

Everyone sat down around the table.

Mya felt the need to begin. To come clean. To spill the beans, or, in this case, the lack of beans. "Before we get started, I'd just like to say—"

"—that this was a combination of the two families," Franko announced talking over Mya. "We all decided that we gonna work together on this."

"Yes," Rita explained. "Instead of making it a contest between Mya and Eric. We thought it should be a family affair."

"We did?" Mya said, glancing over at her mother. Rita threw her a don't-deny-it look, and fortunately for both of them, she caught it. "I mean, we did…work together. On this project. Absolutely. Together. Every single one of us."

"From day one," Grammy added.

"We all get along so well," Rita confirmed. "Always have. Especially Eric and Mya. Ever since they were kids."

Franko coughed and rolled his eyes. Mya saw him, but didn't think anybody else did. She didn't exactly know what everyone was up to, but for the time being, she was glad they were working together, even if it was simply for the benefit of the producers.

Producer John hesitated, but then said, "We heard about what happened at your house, Rita, with the dog destroying your new set, and frankly we were a bit surprised when you didn't phone and cancel this meeting."

"Oh, that. A minor problem. The kitchen is perfect. The new show we taped is fabulous."

"We taped a new show?" Mya asked, while her mom grabbed Mya's leg under the table. A warning shot. Something her mother had done ever since she was a kid whenever Mya was just about to come clean on whatever it was that Rita was trying to hide. It never worked when Mya was a kid, but she decided to heed her mother's warning today. Mya's voice dropped an octave. "Of course, we taped a new show…this morning."

Rita added, "We worked well into the morning, and we're all a little sleepy because of it."

She squeezed Mya's leg again.

"Personally, I loved what I just saw," Producer Dorothy offered. "Especially the scenes with the accordion-playing cops. I'd like to see more of that. You and Eric did a great job, and I, for one, would like to see it continue."

So Mya hadn't gone mental. She actually had heard that miserable accordion.

Mya was floored. She had no idea how this woman could possibly know about that night, unless, of course, Eric had saved something off his laptop.

"Yes. It's perfect. Just the right mix of food and fun. Loved the Frank and Mia wedding dinner," Producer Lex chimed in. "Glad to have you and Eric as part of the team. How did you two ever come up with this stuff?"

Grammy said, "I had a little something to do with that."

Mya shot a disappointed look at her grandmother. *Even Grammy was in on this?*

Mya didn't know how to answer, or what to answer, or even what to think. She had absolutely no idea what he was talking about.

The Frank and Mia wedding dinner?

She tried to remain calm. Tried to think straight. Wanted to keep her cool. She said, "Well, I—"

"It's a hoot! Especially when that white poodle jumped up on the counter and Voodoo just sat there looking at her like she was crazy. Amazing how destructive one dog could be."

"Brenda Lee? It was Brenda Lee who destroyed the kitchen?" Mya gasped. She could hardly contain herself. She needed to know exactly what was going on.

Rita calmly smiled while she pinched Mya's leg.

Mya jumped. "Ouch."

"Is everything all right?" Producer John asked.

"Everything. Yes. Right," Rita stammered. "And I'd like everyone to come over to my house tonight for a pool party. Franko and I will be cooking. It's to celebrate the success of our show and to officially announce our engagement." She smiled over at Franko. "It's going to be a fabulous party."

The producers stood up and everyone shook hands with Franko and Rita. Rita ate it up. It was all very cordial. All very nice, but Mya was all shook up.

"Mom, can I see you out in the hall for just a minute?"

"We'll talk in the car, dear," her mother said while hamming it up for the producers.

Mya pinched her mother's leg. "Ouch!" Rita yelped and shot Mya an offended look.

"Excuse us," Rita said. "We'll be right back."

Mya stood up, grabbed her mother's hand and led her out the door.

"What is going on? What was all that about Brenda Lee? Eric was with me in Vegas, how could he have taped the dogs in your kitchen?" Mya asked once they were out in the hall.

"It's all very complicated, dear. You know I've never been very good with technical stuff. Something about interval taping. You'll have to ask Eric about the details. But they love you. They want you both to be part of the show. I couldn't be happier—"

"That's fine, but how did Brenda Lee get inside the house?"

"Oh, I guess I left the side door open. It was just easier for Voodoo to get in and out. It seemed like the right thing to do at the time. But, like you say, no worries. It all worked out."

Panic. That's what was beginning to set in. Total panic. "So, Eric had nothing to do with the kitchen?"

"Of course not, dear. Eric was with you in Vegas. Remember? Although, you did look rather wasted up on that stage, dancing around that pole. Maybe he shouldn't have used that part of the video. Perhaps you should talk to him about editing that out for the public."

Mya remembered her Vegas trip only too well, and embarrassment flew up her spine to think that those producers had seen her dancing. How would they ever take her seriously again? The man had no sense of privacy. *How could he!*

Of course, she also remembered the roomful of Elvises howling at her.

Oh, what's the difference.

"I thought I destroyed everything when his laptop hit the ground. I've been upset about it ever since it happened. You know that. And now I find out that wasn't the case? I've been fretting over nothing?"

"He found a computer whiz who was able to save *almost* everything. You should turn your phone on once in a while. We tried to call you and tell you what happened. Poor Eric was frantic with worry when we couldn't reach you."

"He was?"

"Well, maybe not frantic, but we were all worried about you. Now, let's go back in the room. Everyone wants to talk to you about the format of our new show. It's so exciting!"

Mya was just about to go back in the room when she remembered an *operative* word in her mother's explanation that needed clarifying. "What does *almost* everything mean?"

"What?"

"You said the computer whiz was able to save *almost* everything. What exactly does that mean?"

"Well, sweetheart, apparently Eric needed more space on his laptop so he moved his thesis onto that DVD and—"

Mya could see it now, rolling around on the driveway, heading straight for that damn thorny cactus.

Shit!

Mya didn't want to hear anything else. Couldn't bear to listen to how wrong she'd been. She turned and ran down the hall with one burning thought.

She had to find Eric.

THERE WAS A SHORT PERIOD of time when Eric thought he should stay and face Mya at the meeting, but that thought quickly faded when he saw her enter the building with Grammy. He knew he was no match for her, from his dumb clothes to his even dumber ideas. He hadn't even waited for the response to the video. The truth be told, he didn't really care. All he wanted to do was get back to Savannah as soon as he could.

There was just one minor problem holding him back. He was in love with Mya and didn't want to let her go.

For the rest of the day, and into the early evening, Eric went shopping. Not just for more cassettes for his camera or another software package like he usually did. No. This time he went shopping for clothes, shoes and a new haircut. He'd gone back to Olga's for the do, which hadn't taken much thought, but finding the perfectly cool outfit was a totally different problem.

He would have liked to have brought Gram along and let her dress him, but if he was going to do this right, he had to do it on his own.

Several hours later, he was dressed for sin. He wore a combination of an Armani navy shirt, Versace black slacks, and Punto Blanco briefs. His shoes were something called Prada Logo Loafers, which he paid way too much for, but the salesgirl assured him Mya would notice.

He bought two hundred-dollar bottles of champagne, the best chocolate-covered strawberries he could find, an assortment of candles, and hiked it all up to the rooftop at Rita's house without any of the pool-party guests noticing.

THERE IT WAS AGAIN, Mya thought as she lay on her bed with the covers over her head. She'd spent the entire afternoon and part of the evening searching for Eric and now all she wanted to do was have a good cry over her miserable self, but somebody from her mother's extremely loud party was messing with her bedroom door.

"Go away," she yelled from under the blankets, but the noise continued. She really didn't want to see anyone, especially not her mother or Grammy. She'd had enough of their sage advice to last her for the rest of her life…thank you very much.

But the annoying sound wouldn't stop. "I don't want to talk to anyone. Please go away," she said, but this time the noise got louder.

The thing about it was, she knew she looked like hell, felt like hell and wanted to wallow in her own misery without somebody telling her that everything would be all right. Because she knew absolutely that everything was not, and never could be, all right again.

She had lost the one guy in the entire world whom she loved with all her heart. The one person she loved for who he was and not what he looked like. All she wanted was to be able to see him one more time. That's all. But he was gone, which said he really didn't love her. That those words he'd used in Vegas were just a mean joke of some kind. It was merely the Elvis suit talking and not Eric.

This time when the knocking sound happened again, she jumped out of bed and went to the door. She couldn't take it anymore. Apparently, whoever it was didn't understand "go away."

Mya had been so upset when she'd returned home without finding Eric that for once in her entire adult life she didn't think about her clothes, hair or makeup. Instead it seemed comforting to slip on a pair of old ratty jeans she found in the bottom of her dresser drawer and a top she'd worn in high school. She had pulled her hair back and tied it with a big floral scrunchy, and she had washed off all her makeup. She looked about as cool as a pair of stretch pants. But the irony about it was, for once in her life, she just didn't care.

Her cell phone rang. She didn't want to pick it up, but when she saw that it was a New York City area code, she thought perhaps it was Grace with a change of heart.

"Hello," she eagerly said, ready to do some major groveling.

"Where are you, babe?"

"I'm…um…Bryan?"

"The one and only. Been thinking about you. Where you been hanging?"

"I'm…in California. At my mom's."

"Well, get your fine butt back here. It's time we made this thing serious."

"We don't have a *thing*." She wondered what she'd ever seen in the man.

"Sure we do, and it's time to do it. Make it legal. All our friends are taking that big step, so why not us?"

"Are you asking me to marry you…on my cell?"

"Yeah. Great, huh?"

"No. Not great."

"Oh. Okay. Not the right approach. Would a text message be better? 'Cause we can do it that way. Or maybe you want a picture of me? Or a short video. Whatever. But doing it on the cell is what's out there right now."

"That's just it. I don't want what's *out there*. I want scrunchies and sweatpants, white suits and accordion music. I want something real. Something true. I'm sorry, Bryan, but—"

"Hey. Don't sweat it. I took my shot. It didn't work out. So…I'll be seeing you around then."

"I—"

He hung up.

The thumping on her door suddenly got louder. She shut her phone, ready to join her mother's party. She knew what she wanted now. She knew who she wanted and, this time, she was ready to do whatever it took to get him back.

Mya grabbed the doorknob and swung the door open, ready to join whoever it was at her mom's party.

But it was Voodoo.

Mya's heart instantly melted as she knelt down to pet the sweet little beast. He felt all warm and loving next to her body. He was really a sweet dog, she just never noticed it before. "Hey, you. Where'd you come from, huh?"

He backed up and let out a huffy bark.

"Okay, is this like a Lassie thing? 'Cause if it is, I get the message. I'm supposed to follow you, right?"

Voodoo ran down the hallway toward the open window. Mya followed right behind him. She was so full of emotion that she didn't know if she should be happy that Eric had sent his dog to fetch her, or nervous over what he wanted to say.

As soon as she stepped out on the roof, she heard music and laughter coming from her mom's party.

"You're not going to believe who Officer Curtis is giving accordion lessons to," Eric said, standing next to the telescope.

"The Kevin Bacon wannabe?"

"How'd you know?"

"Women's intuition."

But the Kevin lookalike wasn't important anymore.

In the moon's glow, for some reason, Eric didn't really look like Eric. "What have you done to your hair?"

"I had it styled. What do you think?"

"Well, I…"

She liked his curly, shaggy hair better.

Then she noticed his clothes. Expensive and ultra-hip. "You look…cool." She took him all in. "Are those Pradas?"

They were like the hottest loafers on the planet.

"Yeah. Thanks. It's the look I was going for." His gaze covered her body. "You look…incredible. Beautiful. Like you're…comfortable." He moved toward her.

"Thanks. It's the look I was going for." She took a couple steps closer to him.

They both started talking at the same time. "I want to—"

They laughed. She loved how his eyes sparkled when he laughed. Actually, she loved everything about the man standing in front of her on their rooftop.

Mya spoke first. "I just want to say that I'm truly sorry I destroyed your tavern DVD. I know how hard you worked and—"

He stopped her. "It doesn't matter. I'm going to use *La Dolce Rita* for my thesis. Because of you, it turned out much better than I could ever have hoped for." He took another step closer. "So, I hear we're going to be working together."

She could feel her body heating up, feel her heart pounding inside her chest.

"That's the plan. Do you have a problem with that?" She took a step toward him. Could she tell him? Could she tell him she loved him and never wanted to be apart from him again?

He shook his head and snickered. "No. I think we work well together. Don't you?"

"Always. Ever since we were kids." She looked into his eyes, thinking that her legs would buckle at any moment. Would he be there to catch her? "There's just one tiny thing."

He was standing so close their heat was palpable. "What's that?" he whispered.

She took a step back to look down at his feet. "We have to get your dad a pair of those shoes for the show. They are the coolest…"

He took her in his arms and she couldn't speak anymore, or think or even stand on her own. She fell into him and he brushed his lips across hers. "I love you, Mya Strano. I always have and always will."

"I love you, Eric Baldini, always have and…"

Eric kissed her with such intensity, if she wasn't holding on tight, she would have floated away. That's when Elvis echoed from the party below.

They both started moving to the music at the same time and Eric fell into his *Rock-a-hula* routine. As Mya twirled and gyrated to the beat, taunting Eric with each sexy move, she could think of only one thing: A permanent, bright pink stripper pole right in the middle of her new L.A. bedroom.

How cool was that?

Voodoo howled.

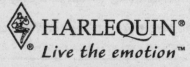

If you enjoyed what you just read,
then we've got an offer you can't resist!

Take 2 bestselling love stories FREE!

Plus get a FREE surprise gift!

HARLEQUIN®
Presents

Seduction and Passion Guaranteed!

Legally wed, but he's never said…
"I love you."

They're…

Wedlocked!

**The series
where
marriages are
made in haste…
and love
comes later…**

**Look out for more Wedlocked! marriage stories
in Harlequin Presents throughout 2005.**

www.eHarlequin.com   HPWL2

HARLEQUIN®
Presents

Seduction and Passion Guaranteed!

The O'CONNELLS

by

Sandra Marton

In order to marry, they've got to gamble on love!

Welcome to the world of the wealthy Las Vegas family the O'Connells. Take Keir, Sean, Cullen, Fallon, Megan and Briana into your heart as they begin that most important of life's journeys—a search for deep, passionate, all-enduring love.

Coming in Harlequin Presents®
April 2005 #2458
Briana's story:
THE SICILIAN MARRIAGE
by *Sandra Marton*

Gianni Firelli is used to women trying to get into his bed. So when Briana O'Connell purposely avoids him, she instantly catches his interest. Briana most definitely does not want to be swept off her feet by any man. Or so she thinks, until she meets Gianni....